"A wife would be very useful to me."

Quinn continued. "Dinner parties, entertaining—it is all so much easier with a hostess. I would make sure you don't lose out on the deal."

"Quinn!" Candy interrupted him before he could say any more. "Quinn, we don't love each other." *Or you don't love me, more to the point.* "It wouldn't work, you must know that," she said with deliberate casualness.

"On the contrary, I think it would work very well. Marriages of convenience are far more successful than so-called love matches."

"So that's what this is, a convenient proposal?" Candy asked flatly.

"I guess." His eyes narrowed and he drew her closer. "But I would satisfy you, Candy, in every way. Have no doubts about that."

Dear Reader,

My husband and I will celebrate our thirtieth wedding anniversary in the new millennium and we're planning something special! It set me to thinking about the day my husband proposed (yes, it was the full works—bended knee, little velvet box holding the ring of my dreams, deep red roses and champagne, the lot!).

Like people, proposals come in all shapes and sizes, which is what makes them—and us—so interesting. Halfway up a mountainside in a blizzard, on a beautiful Caribbean beach, stuck in a broken-down train in the middle of nowhere… I've heard the lot from friends and family over the years.

So, I thought, why not write a special duet of books exploring the motives behind two very special—and very different—proposals in one family? And that's how the idea for MARRY ME? was born: two books on one extremely romantic theme. I do hope you enjoyed *A Suspicious Proposal* last month, and now the sequel, *A Convenient Proposal.*

Lots of love,

Helen Brooks

Helen Brooks

A CONVENIENT PROPOSAL

MARRY ME?

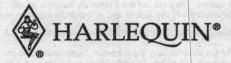

HARLEQUIN®

TORONTO • NEW YORK • LONDON
AMSTERDAM • PARIS • SYDNEY • HAMBURG
STOCKHOLM • ATHENS • TOKYO • MILAN • MADRID
PRAGUE • WARSAW • BUDAPEST • AUCKLAND

ISBN 0-373-12118-0

A CONVENIENT PROPOSAL

First North American Publication 2000.

Copyright © 2000 by Helen Brooks.

This edition published by arrangement with Harlequin Books S.A.

® and TM are trademarks of the publisher. Trademarks indicated with ® are registered in the United States Patent and Trademark Office, the Canadian Trade Marks Office and in other countries.

Visit us at www.eHarlequin.com

Printed in U.S.A.

CHAPTER ONE

CANDY stared at her reflection in the small round mirror in the aeroplane's toilet, and it was with something of a sense of shock that she took in the image peering back at her.

Thick, silky hair of a glowing russet-red hanging in soft waves to slender shoulders, vivid sapphire-blue eyes under finely arched brows, clear, creamy skin dotted with the merest sprinkling of freckles across a small straight nose... It looked like her, admittedly, she thought numbly, and yet how could the pain and frightening bitterness of the last months not show on the face of the girl who gazed back at her?

But she had always been good at hiding her real feelings. The thought brought her small chin up in unconscious defiance of the voice inside her head telling her she couldn't do this, that she should have stayed in Canada where everything was safe and normal, that she wasn't strong enough yet to strike out on her own.

'You are a survivor, Candy Grey.' She brushed back the wispy fringe from her forehead as she spoke out loud, and on realising her hands were trembling she clenched them into fists at her side. 'You *are*.' The azure gaze became a glare that dared her to contradict it. 'And you are going to make it.'

The future might not be what she had imagined for herself this time a year ago, but so what? The narrowed eyes with their abundantly thick lashes were unflinching. She could either wallow in self-pity, and eventually let it drown her, or she could make a new life for herself—a life where *she* called all the shots and where she was answerable to no one. Life on her own terms. She nodded at the declaration, her slim shoulders straightening.

Once back in her comfortable seat in the first-class section of the plane, she ignored the none too subtle overtures from the man in the next seat, who had proved a pain for the whole of the journey from Vancouver, and endeavoured to prepare herself for the landing at Heathrow. Then, once she had battled her way through the terminal, she could pick up the car one of Xavier's business colleagues had arranged to have waiting for her arrival and, bingo, she was on her way, she told herself firmly. And so it proved.

Within a short time of the plane landing she was ensconced in a little blue Fiesta, her luggage filling the boot and back seat and spilling over on to the passenger seat at the side of her.

It took her several attempts to navigate her way out of London but she didn't panic. After the bottomless abyss of the last months what was getting lost in the overall scheme of things? Candy asked herself caustically on eventually finding herself in the outskirts. If nothing else she had learnt what was important and what was not.

Autonomy was important. Being able to choose what she wanted to do and when she wanted to do it. She flexed her long slim legs at the memory of her endless months in the wheelchair and drew in the air very slowly between her small white teeth. She might still get exhausted very quickly, and the self-physiotherapy the doctor had taught her would have to continue for some months yet, but she was mistress of her own destiny again.

And it could have all been so different. The horrendous accident that had taken Harper could so easily have left her in a wheelchair for life. All things considered, she was lucky.

The thought mocked the devastation of what was left of

her life, but Candy reiterated it in her mind almost defiantly. She *was* lucky, she told herself firmly.

She had fought back against the consuming thick grey blanket of depression which had weighed her down in the early days, throwing it off with Herculean resolve. She had climbed out of the dark, mindless pit of that time and she was blowed if she would allow herself to be sucked into it again by self-pity.

And everyone had been so good to her, and still continued to be. Of course they all felt sorry for her, she acknowledged a trifle bitterly. She knew exactly what they'd been saying. The car accident, her fiancé being killed, Candy's struggle to emerge from the coma she had been in for days after the collision only to surface to the realisation that she might never walk again—it was all *terrible*, they'd said soberly. No wonder dear Candy was depressed and apathetic.

And she had let them believe what was convenient. She hadn't told a living soul the real reason for the suicidal emptiness of those early days and she never would.

The strident honking of an oncoming car brought Candy sharply out of the morass of black memories, and, although the other driver's anger was directed at a smart red sports car which had deliberately cut across its path, the incident was enough to nudge her mind fully back to her driving.

The November day was bright but bitterly cold, bare branches of trees reaching out into a silver-blue sky as the car ate up the miles along the pleasant countrified route Candy was following.

It was just after three when she reached the small Sussex town she had been making for, and she was exhausted. She glanced at the carefully written instructions she'd fixed to the dashboard and followed them to the letter. Within ten minutes the car had turned off the tree-lined road of prosperous-looking homes and on to a wide pebbled drive in front of a large, sprawling detached house.

'Veterinary Surgery.' Never had two words looked sweeter. Candy cut the engine, leant back in the seat and stretched her neck, running her hands through her hair before massaging her scalp lightly.

The drive had been a short one compared to the long hauls she was used to making as part of everyday life in Canada, but it was at times like this that her body reminded her—all too stringently—that she wasn't quite so well as she would like to believe.

Still, all she had to do now was collect the key of Essie's cottage from Quinn Ellington, who now owned the practice, and follow his instructions for the last mile or two. Easy. She rotated her head once more and climbed out of the car, walking across the drive to the big old-fashioned oak door and ringing the bell before stepping back a pace.

The seconds ticked by, and after a full minute Candy tried the bell again. And again. When that didn't bring a result she turned the big brass doorknob and stepped gingerly into a large square hall, the white and black tiles on the floor spangled by the autumn sunlight.

The hall was empty, and so was the reception area beyond it, but just as she seated herself somewhat uncertainly in one of the straight-backed upholstered chairs dotted about the bright and cheerful waiting area, a large middle-aged woman popped her head round the door leading from the hall.

'Are you Candy? Xavier's niece?' It was rushed and harassed, and Candy only managed a quick nod—opening her mouth to speak before the woman cut in again with, 'We've got an emergency. I must get back. Wait there and Quinn will be with you as soon as he can.' Then the door closed again and all was quiet.

Great. Candy stared blankly across the space. She hadn't

expected the red carpet treatment or anything like that, but a, Hi, how are you? or a, Nice to meet you, wouldn't have come amiss.

She eased her flat leather shoes off her feet and dug the fingers of both hands into the small of her back, working tense, bunched muscles for some moments before settling back with a tired sigh and shutting her eyes. She might as well relax while she waited, she decided drowsily. No point in getting ruffled. She let her head fall back against the whitewashed wall behind her and was asleep in the next moment.

When Quinn walked into the reception area five minutes later he had the apology hovering on his lips, but instead of a possibly irate or testy young woman confronting him he saw Candy. Fast asleep, her coppery hair in silky disarray, thick eyelashes lying like smudges on the pale cream of a skin that looked to be translucent. Impossibly lovely and quite alarmingly fragile.

He stopped abruptly, ebony eyes narrowing into slits of black light, and he remained like that for a good few seconds before glancing at his watch. Five minutes and she was sleeping the sleep of the dead; she must have been out on her feet. Still, that wasn't surprising. He knew Xavier and Essie had been hotly against this young woman making the journey from Canada alone, but Essie had informed him—ruefully—that Xavier's niece had a lot of her uncle's stubbornness. It was in the genes.

He hadn't expected her to be quite so beautiful; her photo hadn't done her justice. The thought came from nowhere and Quinn brushed it aside irritably, his strong, chiselled face hardening. This was Xavier's niece and she had been through hell; whether she was beautiful or not was irrelevant. She needed peace and quiet and looking after, although the last was to be done without her knowledge. But he'd promised Xavier and Essie he would keep an eye on this young woman and he would. In a fatherly fashion.

He glanced again at the lovely face, the dusky red lips lying slightly open in a small pout, and felt his senses stir before he turned sharply, making his way through the heavy fire door into the rear of the building and walking to the end of a long corridor, into the surgery's neat, shining kitchen.

Marion was in there, her plump, good-natured face flushed and perspiring. 'The coffee's nearly ready.'

'She's asleep.' He inclined his head towards the door. 'But thanks anyway. I'll take the tray through in a minute and wake her up. And thanks for helping out too; it would happen today of all days.'

They had just dealt with the canine victim of a road accident, and due to the fact Quinn had sent his two assistant vets out on calls, and the practice nurse was off ill with flu, there had only been Marion—his very able but slightly squeamish receptionist—to assist whilst he conducted the emergency operation the dog's injuries had necessitated. But all had gone well and that was the main thing.

Marion smiled at him now, nodding at his face as she said, a touch of laughter in her voice, 'Wipe the blood off first, eh? You're liable to frighten the poor girl to death like that.'

Quinn flicked a glance at himself in the square triangle of mirror above the sink as he muttered, 'Damn it.' He wiped the blood off his cleft chin and one hard, angular cheekbone before raking back a lock of jet-black hair off his forehead with his damp hands and making an effort to smooth down the rest of his unruly locks. 'I need a haircut.'

'I've been telling you that for weeks,' said Marion with a motherly sigh. The trouble was, Quinn couldn't care less about his appearance, she thought fondly. Considering the quite shattering ruthless attractiveness of the man that

'Homemade,' he countered breezily. 'Marion looks on herself as a surrogate mother as well as my receptionist, and she's made it her life's mission to feed me up.'

Candy bit her lip and looked straight at him, her vivid blue eyes narrowing. 'Essie has asked you to look out for me, hasn't she?'

She was nothing if not straightforward, thought Quinn appreciatively. He liked that in a person; it was a rare quality these days. Of course he could dodge the question he knew she was asking, but her directness deserved better than that.

'Yes.' It was equally forthright, and as he settled back in his chair, his ebony eyes holding her gaze and his long legs stretched out before him, Candy felt something tighten in her stomach. An awareness, a pulse, a throb of something she hadn't felt in a long, long time, and it scared her to death.

'Well, you needn't bother,' she said flatly. 'I'm not a child and I don't appreciate being treated like one.'

No, whatever else, she certainly wasn't a child, Quinn thought, as her scent—something delicate and elusive—drifted towards him as she rose abruptly.

'There's something wrong with people looking out for each other?'

He hadn't moved, and his voice was still relaxed and cool, but suddenly there was an element to his maleness that she hadn't been aware of before. An authority, something imperious and cold that told her she was being stupid. And it hit her on a raw place.

'No, of course not,' she shot back sharply, 'if that's what they want. But I don't want it; that's the point.'

'And you don't think it's perfectly understandable that Xavier doesn't want Essie worrying about you at such a vulnerable time in her pregnancy?' Quinn asked silkily.

Oh, nice one. She stared at him, her eyes widening with

shock at being put in her place so adroitly. In one fell
swoop he had accused her of being childish and selfish and
ungrateful without voicing any of those things. There was
a lot more to this man than met the eye, but then she had
suspected that the minute she had set eyes on him. What
you saw was not what you got with Mr Quinn Ellington,
she told herself caustically. Mr Nice Guy when it suited
him, but that was all.

'I shall stay in touch with them,' she said defiantly.

'That's very good of you.' It was deeply sarcastic.

Her nostrils flared and she would have loved to have
made a grand exit, but she didn't have the key or the instructions.

'Sit down, Candy, and finish your coffee.' It was an order, not an invitation.

'I would prefer to leave now, if I can have the key?'
Why was she behaving like this? Candy asked herself in
disbelief. Even the note in her voice wasn't really her. She
was never petulant.

'Sit down.' It was a bark this time, and she sat, acknowledging, with a touch of dark humour, that he was certainly
in the right profession. There wasn't an animal alive that
would step out of line if he spoke to it like that. Well, she
needed the key and so she would play along, but once she
had it she would make sure she never set eyes on Mr Quinn
Ellington again. Essie or no Essie!

'Thank you.' Quinn wasn't sure if he was angrier with
himself or this Titian-haired virago who looked like an angel but had the temper of something from the other place.
But she was Essie's fledgling, she was still recovering from
the sort of accident that no one got out of alive, she was
all alone in an alien country and he had promised to look
out for her, damn it. He had promised. And he hadn't lost
his temper for years; why had he to start with her, now?
He took a deep breath and forced his mouth out of the grim

line it had set in. 'Now, please drink your coffee; you look ready to drop and it will help you concentrate on the drive to the cottage.'

Oh, so she was an inept driver now as well? Candy scowled at him, her eyes shooting blue sparks that negated any idea she was sleepy. But she finished the coffee and ate the finger of shortbread Quinn had wedged on the saucer. It was delicious, and she would have loved another slice, but she would rather have been hung, drawn and quartered than say so.

'Ready?' Quinn rose as he spoke, and it dawned on her he was tall, very tall. He towered over her five feet eight by at least six inches, and he needed a haircut. Her eyes widened slightly as the thought hit and she pushed it aside firmly. She didn't care if his hair grew down to his feet; it was no concern of hers if that quiff kept falling in his eyes.

'I'll meet you round the front.'

She had been hesitating on how to finish the meeting. It seemed a bit fatuous to thank him for the coffee, but she couldn't very well just ask for the key again. Now, as Quinn spoke, she found herself gaping at him before she shut her mouth with a little snap. So he was still determined to escort her to the cottage? She swallowed back the hot retort that had jumped to her lips and almost choked with the effort, before sweeping past him and wrenching open the front door.

Calm down, Candy; don't let him get to you. She stood for a moment on the doorstep and breathed deeply of the crisp, cold English air before striding over to the Fiesta and unlocking the door.

Once inside the car she started the engine and then waited. Within moments a sleek, beautiful champagne-coloured Aston Martin nosed on to the front drive from the back of the house. It figured. She allowed a small cynical smile to play round her angry mouth. This was a car women would take a second and a third glance at, and she didn't doubt that was why Quinn had bought it.

Oh, why was she being so bitchy? she asked herself in the next moment, as Quinn raised a hand in acknowledgment before easing the car past the docile little Fiesta. He was entitled to drive any car he liked!

Harper had liked powerful cars. The statement was in answer to her previous thoughts, and she recognised it as such as she followed Quinn out on to the main road. The realisation made her nip at her lower lip. No, she wasn't going to do this. She wasn't going to get all bitter and twisted and tar all men with the same brush. No doubt there were still a few men out there, nice, ordinary men, who were capable of being faithful all their lives. The thought was without conviction, and she frowned at herself before shrugging irritably.

It didn't matter one way or the other anyway. She didn't intend to fall into the trap of commitment and all that hogwash ever again, so it was pointless to think along these lines. She clamped her lips together, straightened her back and followed Quinn into the sort of narrow country lane that was pure picture book England.

They passed several huge thatched cottages with magnificently laid out gardens, and within a moment or two the lane had narrowed still more to show green fields either side of the drystone walls.

Candy was just thinking she hoped they didn't meet any traffic from the opposite direction when Quinn's indicator began to flash and his snail's pace slowed still more, before he eased the Aston Martin into a pull-in just big enough to take two cars.

'Oh, Essie...' Candy spoke out loud, as though Xavier's wife was in the car with her, but her first sight of the cottage Essie still couldn't bear to sell was enchanting.

It was tiny, minute, but the narrow winding path that led

to the gnarled front door, the pretty front garden, the white-painted exterior and quaint leaded windows under their bonnet of thatch were chocolate-box material.

The cottage looked to have masses of ground at the back, and she could imagine the gardens would be a blaze of colour come the spring, but even now, with the bare branches of the trees silhouetted against the dying gold sky, the vista was breathtaking. She could understand now why Essie had hung on to her little corner of English heaven, even though Xavier had a penthouse in London for when he was over on business. If this was hers she wouldn't sell it. No way.

And she was allowed to stay here as long as she liked—Essie had been adamant about that. 'Months, a year, two years, for ever,' Xavier's wife had said airily when she had first offered Candy the sanctuary. 'Make it yours, Candy. It's the perfect spot to resume your painting and it's great to think of the place being used again. Xavier arranged for a lady to dust and air the place every so often, and there's a gardener who keeps the outside under control, but other than them you won't see a living soul unless you want to.'

The last words stayed with her now, as she opened the car door and looked over to where Quinn was holding the rickety garden gate open for her.

'Come in and have a nose round first and then I'll get your cases,' he said evenly, but without a smile.

'There's really no need. I can manage perfectly well—'

'And then I'll get out of your hair,' he cut in with cool aplomb. 'Okay?'

She ought to say she hadn't meant she was waiting for him to leave. It was the polite thing, the courteous thing to do. But she *had* meant just that and she wasn't going to lie. Candy raised her chin a notch or two, nodded brightly, and walked over to the gate. She had to brush past him to get through, and as she did so the smell of him, a mixture of delicious aftershave and something lemon, teased her nostrils, making her senses jump.

It didn't help either that he seemed even bigger and darker than before, in the heavy black leather jacket he had pulled on over his working denims, or that the muscled strength that padded his shoulders and chest was intimidatingly close.

She concentrated on walking to the front door with every ounce of her will, and by the time she reached it she was able to stand aside and let Quinn open the door for her with the magic key without a tremor. A few more minutes and then she would be alone. She could kick her shoes off her aching feet, have a long soak in a hot tub and fall into bed. That was all she wanted. Exploring, shopping for groceries, everything else could wait until tomorrow. She had never felt so exhausted in all her life.

The interior of the cottage was everything the outside promised and more. Polished wood floors, beamed ceilings, whitewashed walls with one or two good paintings—it was perfect, Candy decided happily.

The open-plan sitting room and tiny kitchen had stairs leading upstairs to the cottage's bedroom and diminutive bathroom and furniture was at a minimum—just a rich deep red sofa and two easy chairs, a nest of small occasional tables, a tiny bookcase tucked under the window and two bar stools standing under the little breakfast bar which separated the kitchen from the sitting room.

There was no TV, no microwave—although a hardy stove dominated the kitchen space—no fridge and no washing machine.

'I've had the telephone reconnected.' Quinn indicated the phone resting on the top of the nest of tables. 'And the fire's ready to light. There are more logs and coal stored in the old potting shed at the back of the cottage and a list of everyone—doctor, dentist, coalman et cetera—pinned to the inside of the top cupboard.'

'Oh, right, thank you.' Candy was beginning to feel like a worm. There were fresh flowers in a vase on the bookcase, and when she opened a couple of the kitchen cupboards they were full of food. The bread bin held a crusty loaf, there was a box containing fruit and vegetables on the breakfast bar, at the side of which stood a pack of thick steaks, bacon, eggs and other produce, including a couple of bottles of very good wine. She took a deep breath and asked, 'Did...did *you* get everything in?'

Quinn shrugged. 'No problem. I didn't think you'd want to shop your first afternoon.'

'How much do I owe you?' she asked jerkily, her cheeks fiery red.

'Don't be ridiculous,' he said shortly.

'Oh, but I must pay you.'

'I said don't be ridiculous.' This time it was accompanied by a scowl that brooked no argument, before he swung round and walked over to the tiny stone fireplace, reaching up for the box of matches on the wooden mantelpiece above and flicking a match to the coals and wood in the grate. 'It's a bit chilly now, but it will soon warm up,' he said quietly. 'There's no central heating, so it's advisable to make sure you don't run out of fuel.'

There was a small, fraught silence while Candy wondered whether to press the matter of payment for the supplies, but she found she didn't dare. 'Thank you,' she said again.

'There's a TV point if you want to get one. Essie never liked the idea herself.'

'Neither do I,' Candy said quickly. 'I shall be painting most of the time anyway, and I love to read, especially in front of a real fire.'

'A homebody?' Jet-black eyes wandered over the slim,

expensively dressed and beautifully coiffured figure in front
of him and a thick black eyebrow rose derisively. It made
Candy want to hit him.

'Actually, I am,' she affirmed tightly.

'Right.'

Candy reminded herself about the food and the flowers
and the fire now burning brightly in the grate and swallowed hard.

'I'll get your cases in.' There was something in the silky
voice that told her he was well aware of the restraint she
had just employed and had relished it.

She went exploring upstairs while Quinn brought her
things in, and found the bedroom, with its pretty drapes and
matching bedspread and leaded window under the eaves,
delightful. There was no wardrobe or dressing table—Essie
had warned her about the makeshift bar she had nailed to
the wall which she had intended to replace with a wardrobe
one day—but Candy didn't mind that. She could perhaps
buy a small pine wardrobe to match the bed, she thought
to herself, and a few other things for Essie before she left.
She'd see how the painting went. She had a list of contacts
from her agent in Canada and several had appeared hopeful.

'Do you want these cases upstairs?'

Upstairs? The thought of Quinn in the bedroom was
enough to send her scurrying down the bare wood stairs
with more speed than was advisable, considering their
steepness. 'No, it's all right,' she said breathlessly as she
almost collided into him at the bottom of the stairs. 'I'll
sort things out later.'

'Leave it to tomorrow, if you can; it must have been a
long day.' She had looked like a young kid for a moment
as she'd galloped down those stairs, but a kid with deep
bruised shadows under her eyes and a soft mouth that was
drooping with tiredness. He'd noticed she limped slightly
too; it was barely discernible, but it was there.

Quinn's thoughts made his smile warm and open as he held out his hand. 'Goodbye, Candy,' he said softly. 'If there's anything you need don't hesitate to call.'

Candy hesitated for a moment, and then she carefully placed her small paw in his big fingers as she said, 'Thank you. I mean that. I didn't mean to be rude earlier, but it's just that I want to be left alone.' And then, realising that was insulting in itself, she groaned inwardly, adding quickly, 'What I mean is—'

'You mean you want the space to breathe.'

He was still holding her hand, his dark head slightly bent towards hers, but it was the note of something undefinable rather than the actual words that brought her startled blue eyes into line with his ebony gaze. She didn't like the feel of what his hard, warm flesh was doing to her, or the fact that she knew she ought to pull away and couldn't. But the knowledge that he knew how she was feeling, *really* knew, had shocked her into immobility.

She ran the tip of her tongue over her lips and saw him follow the motion with his eyes, and the warmth it engendered was enough warning for her to be able to say, 'Yes, that is what I mean,' her voice guarded now.

'Just don't cut yourself off so completely it becomes impossible to take up the reins again.' His voice carried a roughness now, a huskiness that increased the warmth tenfold.

Did he know how sexy he was? she asked herself before she was aware what she was thinking. She didn't think she had ever met anyone with such naked magnetism in all her life.

'I've no intention of doing that,' she said shakily. 'I'm going to work here, at my painting. I've already got the possibility of an exhibition in London if my agent can fix it up, and—'

'I wasn't talking about work.' Suddenly her hand was

free, and ridiculously she felt bereft. 'I'm talking about here, inside.' He touched the black leather over his heart. 'There comes a point where feeling dies—take it from one who knows—and once it's gone it can't be resurrected.'

He was talking about himself. Candy stared at him. She wasn't at all sure how they had reached this point, but suddenly she knew he was talking about himself.

'You tell yourself that one day you'll perhaps take a chance again, open up, get back into the game, and then after a time you wake up one morning and realise you're self-sufficient. You don't need anyone.' His eyes were granite hard now, and inward-looking.

'Surely that's good?' she asked faintly.

Her voice seemed to bring him back to the present and he blinked once, a mask covering his face as he said, his voice remote, 'Maybe, maybe not. Who knows?' The brief moment of intimacy was over.

Candy remained where she was as Quinn walked to the front door, but once he had opened it and stepped out into the bitingly cold air, in which the odd desultory snowflake was beginning to whirl and dance, she followed him to the doorway and watched him walk down the narrow garden path in the grey twilight.

'Goodbye, Candy.' He turned at the gate, raking back his hair as he said, 'I might make the odd phone call to check you're still in the land of the living, but I promise no house calls. Okay?'

'Okay.'

It was what she had wanted, and she couldn't have made it any plainer, so why did she feel so wretched now? Candy asked herself as she watched him back the Aston Martin out into the lane.

She was tired; that was what it was. And the day had been full of different impressions and images—she wasn't thinking straight.

She raised her hand once as he left, but he didn't glance her way.

Fine. She bit down hard on her lip and then closed the front door and turned to survey her new home. The breakfast bar was still piled high with food, and then she saw the little note he must have scribbled while she had been upstairs. It was propped next to an opened bottle of red wine and it read, 'Have a couple of glasses while you cook the steak. The salad's all ready. Q.'

She drank the first glass sitting in front of the crackling fire, and she was fighting back the tears without having any idea why she wanted to cry. After putting the steak on a low grill she took the second glass up to the bathroom with her and sipped it while she soaked the aches and pains of the long journey away.

It was dark when she tottered downstairs again, and it was really snowing outside, thick, heavy fat flakes blotting out the view beyond the window. She drew the thick red curtains, dished up the steak and salad and poured herself another glass of wine in a spirit of recklessness before throwing another couple of logs on the fire.

She loathed men! She bit into the steak and felt the juice dribble down her chin. She did, she loathed them all. And she *was* going to do exactly what she had made up her mind to do weeks ago in Canada. Concentrate on her painting, forge a career for herself, both here and across the Atlantic, and make her work her life. She knew where she was with paint and paper. They didn't lie, they didn't run away and leave her, she could trust them.

She finished the steak and salad, drained the glass, took a long, hard deep breath and headed for the stairs. The dishes, along with the unpacking could wait for tomorrow.

And nothing—*nothing*—had changed.

CHAPTER TWO

WHEN Candy awoke the next morning it was to a hushed, silent world that was all ethereal whiteness and silver skies. And it was beautiful. It was so, so beautiful.

She stood at the bedroom window as wonder touched her soul and her fingers itched for her canvas and paints for the first time in months. Over a year, in fact.

She skipped her usual morning shower, padding downstairs and finding the suitcase that contained leggings and a thick jumper before hoisting her hair into a high ponytail on top of her head. She didn't even bother to wash her face.

After a hasty breakfast of toast and coffee she unzipped the case holding her paints and other equipment—ignoring the rest piled in one corner where Quinn had left them, which were demanding attention—and after reorganising the layout of the sitting room to give her maximum light she set to work on the images that had burnt themselves on her mind first thing that morning.

At four o'clock, as the light began to fade rapidly, she emerged from the frenzy which had gripped her all day and realized the cottage was freezing and she was starving hungry.

Once the fire was blazing she cooked herself the rest of the steak and finished off the bottle of wine before selecting a book from Essie's bookcase and curling up on the sofa until ten o'clock. A hot bath, a mug of cocoa and she was in bed at half past and dead to the world a minute later.

It was another five days before empty cupboards drove her out to get supplies, but at least she had phoned Essie and Xavier and unpacked by then. And she had the makings of a terrific picture too, she told herself, as she persuaded the reluctant Fiesta up the snow-packed lane and out on to the main road towards the town a few miles away.

She had to pass Quinn's veterinary practice on the way into town but she didn't glance at it, not even for a moment.

He hadn't phoned.

And that was fine, perfect, *wonderful*. Sure it was. It meant he had listened to what she had said and received the message loud and clear. And she wasn't going to acknowledge the little voice at the back of her mind that kept nagging as to the reason for the bitterness evident in his voice and face either. His past was his own affair, as was hers.

Had Essie told Quinn anything about her? It was another thought which had been popping up fairly frequently over the last five days.

She hoped not. Not that she had anything to be ashamed of, she told herself militantly; it was just her business, that was all. Her grandmother being the town's tramp, which had caused her mother, Natalie, to be raped by one of her grandmother's unsavoury 'friends' when her mother had been a child of fourteen wasn't exactly the normal family background people expected. Her poor mother... She thought of the photograph Xavier had given her when she was a young girl which was all she had to remind her she had ever had a mother.

Her mother had died giving birth to her. She had found that very hard to come to terms with, in spite of Xavier's gentleness and tenderness when he had told her. And Natalie had been just fifteen years old. Although the tragedy had jolted her grandmother out of her life of dissipation until she died, eight years later, the damage had been done, but Xavier had fought their reputation every inch of the way.

Of course, once he had made his first million nothing had ever been said openly any more. Candy's soft mouth twisted cynically. But in her home town there had still been men who knew the family history and thought they were on to a good thing with her. Not that she had ever told Xavier; he would have knocked them into next week. He had virtually brought her up and she was to all intents and purposes a daughter in her uncle's eyes.

Her background was one of the reasons why she had thought Harper was so wonderful; he had respected her, he had treated her as though she was a piece of precious Meissen porcelain.

She forced her mind away from Harper. How could she have been so naive, so trusting, so utterly pathetic and *dumb*? No, it didn't matter now. She breathed deeply, willing the sick feeling that always accompanied his name to die. Harper was gone, killed in a mass of twisted metal that had borne no resemblance to the car it had been once it had finished rolling down the mountainside.

She was now on the borders of the small Sussex town, and on entering the main street a minute or two later she spied a parking slot to one side of the ancient cobbled marketplace and took it quickly, before she lost the chance.

It was a tight squeeze between a large four-by-four on one side and a badly parked BMW on the other, which was probably why it was still vacant when everywhere else was packed. However, Xavier had taught her to drive in the acres of ground surrounding his lovely home in Vancouver when she'd barely been out of pigtails, and he had coached her so well she could virtually park on a postage stamp.

Manoeuvring completed, she cut the engine, carefully wriggled out of the door and turned to look about her—straight into a pair of dark approving black eyes.

'Very nice.' Quinn indicated the Fiesta with a wave of

his hand as he grinned at her. 'Do all Canadian women drive like you?'

Candy had frozen. He was standing inches from her and he was even bigger and darker than she remembered, and undeniably drop-dead gorgeous, from the top of his raven head to the soles of his muddy boots. And he *was* muddy. Filthy, in fact.

'Hallo, Quinn.' It was late, but better than nothing.

'Hallo, Candy.' It was very serious, but his eyes were smiling. And then, as a number of dogs in the big four-by-four began to bark and yap at the sound of his voice, he shouted, 'Quiet, the lot of you,' and it worked like magic.

'This is yours?' Candy asked in surprise.

'My working vehicle,' he said easily. 'The farmers would think I'd lost it if I turned up in the Aston Martin.'

'Yes, yes, I suppose they would.' Keep talking, act naturally, forget the fact you aren't wearing any make-up and your hair needs washing. 'And the dogs...?'

'All mine.' There was a warmth in his voice as he glanced at the furry heads and bright eyes staring interestedly out of the back of the big vehicle. 'I've had them about eight months now, five in all.'

'*Five?*' she queried brightly, ignoring her pounding heart.

'Bit of story attached to them, I guess. There used to be an old lady in the town who had a little sanctuary for strays, and when she died unexpectedly these five were the ones who weren't taken when we appealed for owners for the inmates. So...'

'You took them when time ran out?' Candy said quietly. She didn't like the story, or, more to the point, she didn't like what it did to her. She didn't want to think of Quinn as the sort of man who would care for the vulnerable and helpless. She didn't want to think of Quinn at all!

He shrugged. 'I was ready for some company, that's all,

and they're a good bunch on the whole, although the little Jack Russell throws his weight about a bit.'

She stared at him. He was playing it down but he loved those dogs; she could see it in his face and hear it in his voice. Candy's own voice was remote and somewhat toneless when she said, 'Well, I must be going. Nice to see you again.'

'Likewise.' His voice was cool now, and outdid hers in tonelessness.

She nodded at him, furious with herself that he made her want to take to her heels and run like the wind on the one hand and on the other... She wanted to remain here, talking to him like this and finding out more and more about him for the rest of the day. Which was plain stupid. Worse, downright dangerous. He was too good-looking, too charismatic, too...*everything* to mess with. Just like Harper.

She was conscious of his eyes on the back of her neck as she walked towards the first of the row of shops at the side of the marketplace, but she didn't look back, and when she came out of the greengrocer's some five minutes later the four-by-four was gone and in its place was an inoffensive little Mini.

The sky suddenly seemed greyer, and she was conscious of the icy wind cutting through her ski-jacket as she stood staring over the marketplace. And then she turned, very sharply, as though she was throwing something off, and made for the next shop, her shoulders straight and her head high.

It snowed again that night, and by morning the wind was working up to a blizzard, but inside the cottage all was warm and snug. Candy had learnt to bank down the fire each night to keep the downstairs of the cottage warm for morning, and when she first rose emptied the previous day's ashes into the big tin bucket she had found hidden under the sink before she poked the fire into a blaze again and put fresh coal and logs on the burgeoning flames.

By mid-afternoon the coal scuttle was empty and the last of the logs was on the fire; it was time to visit the potting shed once more.

Candy pulled on her boots and bright warm ski-jacket and trudged round to the back of the cottage with her head down against the wind, which was driving the snow before it in fierce gusts, and after the routine fight with the aged door of the potting shed she had stepped into the relative sanctuary of its dank dryness.

After filling the coal scuttle and lugging it back to the cottage she returned with the sack for the wood, but it was as she reached for the first log that she heard it. The faintest cry, almost a squeak. Mice? *Rats?* She froze, her heart thudding. Mice she could tolerate, but rats? Their teeth were a little too large and sharp for comfort. Still, if she didn't bother them they probably wouldn't bother her.

She was actually bending to reach for the log again when the sound came once more. It wasn't a squeak, she told herself silently. It was a miaow, a faint mew. There must be a cat in here, but how had it got in and when, and where was it from? She tried, 'Puss, puss, puss,' but to no avail.

Was it hurt or just sheltering from the cold? After some five minutes, when she was getting more and more chilled, she was just on the point of leaving to fetch a saucer of warm milk when a third mew brought her on all fours to peer along the back of the potting shed behind the six-foot pile of stacked logs. And then she saw them. It looked as though there was the smallest hole in one corner, where a couple of bricks had crumbled away, but it had been enough for the mother cat to creep in to give birth to her kittens. And they were tiny, minute, they couldn't be more than a few days old at most, and the she-cat wasn't moving.

Don't let it be dead. Oh, please, don't let it be dead.

Candy stared in horror at the pathetic little scene and then, as one of the three kittens squirmed a little and made the mewing sound again, she looked at the great pile of wood apprehensively. If she attempted to move it, it might fall on the little family and squash them, but she couldn't just leave them here to die either.

How long had it been since the mother cat had had food or water? It could be hours or days; she had no way of knowing.

Quinn. He was a vet. He would know what to do. She was halfway back to the cottage in the next breath, and once inside she opened the cupboard and looked for his number. She knew it was there; she had looked for it on her first morning in England whilst assuring herself she would never, ever use it. It was halfway down the list of emergency numbers—'Quinn Ellington, Veterinary Surgeon.'

She dialled the number with shaking hands, finding she was more upset than she had realised. But there was something so pitiable about the mother cat's valiant attempt to find shelter and safety for her kittens and the way she was lying curled round the minute little scraps to keep them warm.

It was Marion who answered the telephone, and Candy cut through all the social niceties when she said urgently, 'This is Candy, Xavier's niece. I have to speak to Quinn; it's an emergency.'

'Candy?' When she heard Quinn's deep voice after a brief pause she found, ridiculously, that she had to fight for control against the tears welling up in her throat.

'Oh, Quinn. There's a cat in my potting shed and it's not moving and I can't reach it and it's had kittens—'

'Whoa, whoa.' The interruption was firm but gentle. 'Slowly, nice and slowly. Start at the beginning.'

And so she did, and after she had related it all there was

another brief pause before he said, 'It sounds like time is of the essence, so I'd better not wait until evening surgery is finished. Jamie and Bob will have to split my patients between them; it can't be helped. It'll take me a few minutes to fill them in on a couple of the more complicated cases and then I'll get going. I'll be with you in ten…fifteen minutes. All right?'

'The…the lane is full of snow. I don't know if you'll be able to—'

'No problem,' he interrupted her abruptly, but she didn't mind. 'The four-by-four will take care of it. Goodbye for now.' And the phone went dead.

For the next fifteen minutes Candy darted between the front gate and the potting shed some three or four times, but the female cat hadn't moved or opened its eyes, and by the time Quinn's Landrover Discovery eased its way into the pull in she was convinced it was dead.

She all but leapt on Quinn at the garden gate, actually taking his sleeve and hurrying him along the path until his quizzical gaze made her realise what she was doing.

'Oh, I'm sorry.' She dropped her hand from his jacket as though it was red-hot, flushing hotly. But she had never been so pleased to see anyone in her life.

Quinn's big body seemed to fill the potting shed, and after he had squatted down on his heels and peered behind the assembled logs his face became grim. 'We've got to get them out of here, but you're right; it's too risky to try and move this lot unless we absolutely have to. If I can get round the back of the shed I might just be able to reach in the hole where she came in and pull them out one by one that way.'

Candy stared at him doubtfully. The potting shed was in a nice sheltered position, tucked away behind the cottage, but it was completely surrounded on three sides by bushes and vegetation. Whatever way you looked at this it seemed like mission impossible. 'You'd never manage it,' she said mournfully. 'It's not possible.'

He turned from his contemplation of the cat and kittens and then rose to his feet. 'Those last three words are not in my vocabulary,' he said shortly, 'and I'm surprised they're in yours.'

Candy was stung. 'What does that mean?'

'You're a gutsy lady, and gutsy ladies don't give up before they've even started.'

Gutsy? What did that mean? What had Essie told him? Candy didn't stop to think before she voiced her thoughts, and none too gently. 'What do you know about me?' she asked sharply. 'What has Essie said?'

'Essie?' Quinn looked genuinely surprised. 'Essie hasn't said anything beyond the fact that you wanted a break for a few months? Why, what should she have said?'

'Nothing.' In spite of the zero temperatures outside Candy was hot now. Her and her big mouth. But it was him—he seemed to bring out the worst in her.

Quinn continued to hold her wary gaze for a moment more before he said, his voice even, but with an edge that spoke of irritation, 'I merely meant that to take the decision to uproot yourself and come to pastures new after the sort of accident you've been recovering from took some guts. Okay? Nothing more, nothing less. If you've a whole host of skeletons in your particular cupboard I couldn't care less, Candy.'

Well, that put her in her place, didn't it?

'But what I do care about is trying to get this cat and her kittens in a position where I can make an examination, and as quickly as possible. Clear?'

'Perfectly.' She glared at him.

'Right. Now, I'm going to go round the back and see what I can do and I want you to remain here and keep an eye on them. If you see my hand come through give a yell and we'll go from there, with you directing me. Do you understand?'

'Of course I understand,' she shot back tightly. 'I'm not stupid.'

'No one said you were, Candy.' He was employing the same tone with her as he would with a difficult animal, she just *knew* it, and she couldn't remember when something had rankled more. Impossible man! Impossible, insufferable, annoying...

She stood to one side as he made to pass her, and then when he paused in front of her she raised her gaze to his face. He was close, very close. There was barely room for one let alone two in the potting shed, and Quinn was a big man.

He was studying her with an air of quizzical amusement that turned his face into hard angles and planes and made him twice as attractive. She felt her heart give one mighty flip and despised herself for it, but his flagrant masculinity was something that her hormones just didn't seem able to ignore. In fact she doubted if any female would be able to ignore Quinn Ellington.

'What?' she asked aggressively.

'I should have known when I saw that wonderful hair that you'd be a fireball,' he said musingly.

Wonderful hair? He thought she had wonderful hair? She found she couldn't dwell on that, with him so close and those devastating thickly lashed eyes looking into hers. 'I'm not,' she said weakly. 'Not really. It's just that...'

'What?' He folded his arms over his chest and her senses screamed.

'You always seem to press the wrong button,' she managed fairly stiffly.

'Is that so?' He didn't seem too put out by the accusation as his dark glittering gaze moved over her upturned face and rich red hair, in which the melted snow hung in small crystal droplets, and his words were added confirmation of this. He smiled slowly before opening the door and stepping outside, throwing over his shoulder, 'It's better than not hitting any buttons at all.'

Arrogant swine. She stood staring at the empty doorway for a moment or two as she heard him making his way round to the back of the potting shed, and then, remembering his instructions, she knelt down and peered along the grimy, dusty floor.

There was a great deal of muttered cursing in the next few minutes, along with scrabbling and the sound of breaking twigs and branches, but eventually Candy saw a large hand inch cautiously into the small hole. 'You're there! I can see your fingers,' she called quickly.

'Right. Before I do anything else bring that sack round you were going to use for the logs,' came the muffled response. 'And the light's failing fast. Have you got a torch?'

'There is one, but I've been meaning to replace the batteries...'

'Great.' It was caustic. 'Then you'll have to go to the car and get mine; the door's not locked. It's in the back somewhere; you'll need it to keep an eye on things from inside.'

By the time Candy scrambled round to the back of the shed with the torch and the sack it was nearly dark and the snow was falling in ever-increasing gusts. She saw the reason for Quinn's ill-humour when she reached him, or what she could see of him, because only the backs of his legs were visible. He was lying under a vicious hawthorn bush which had been allowed to take over that part of the garden along with some other shrubs and thicket.

'Are you all right?' she proffered tentatively as she pushed the sack forwards.

There was a meaningful pause before, 'I'm not going to even answer that. This damn bush has ripped me apart.'

'Oh, I'm sorry.'

It shouldn't be funny, and it wasn't, not really, but she couldn't help thinking that the man who had sailed out of the potting shed was slightly different from the one stuck under the hawthorn.

Once she was back in place in the potting shed and shining the torch along the floor she directed operations quite successfully.

Quinn was grunting and groaning, but he managed to get the three tiny kittens out fairly easily; it was the mother cat who proved a problem. She had stirred slightly when Quinn extricated her babies, but when he tried to ease her out by her back legs she suddenly found a burst of strength and dug her claws into the side of a log. There followed a careful tug of war before she seemed to fall comatose again, and then, with a little delicate manoeuvring, she followed her kittens.

Candy raced round to the back of the shed, shining the torch on Quinn's legs as he slowly, very slowly, edged backwards with the sack half cradled under his arms. The hawthorn bush didn't want to let go of its prize gracefully and there were more growls of pain and irritation before he was finally sitting upright with the sack in front of him.

'Oh, Quinn.' She was mortified at the sight of him. His face and his hands were ripped and bleeding and the back of his jacket, which had taken the brunt of the hawthorn's unrelenting attack, was in shreds. 'Oh, I am sorry.'

'What?' And then, as he realised what she had meant, 'Don't worry about a couple of scratches; let's get this little lot inside and see what's what. I put my case down in the potting shed; bring it in, would you?'

Once in the warm cottage, Quinn carefully put the rough sack down on the thick rug in front of the blazing fire and they gently opened it up to reveal the sorry little quartet.

Now, in the bright light, they could see the female cat

was a pretty little tortoiseshell, but just skin and bones, and the only time she lifted her head to see what was going on was when Quinn removed the kittens one by one to examine them and they mewed a plaintive protest at being taken from the smell and warmth of their mother.

'They're only a few days old; their eyes aren't open yet,' Quinn muttered as he placed each of the tiny felines into the cardboard box Candy had brought her groceries home in. 'But they all seem pretty healthy, although they're alive with fleas. Let's have a look at Mum.'

Candy sat back on her heels and watched Quinn as his big hands moved tenderly over the pathetic creature, his brow wrinkled as his battle-scarred bloody fingers carefully probed and prodded. The cat made no objection to his inspection, indeed it hardly seemed aware of its surroundings, apart from the several glances at the box where the kittens were still verbally making their displeasure known.

'Well, it isn't feline enteritis.'

His voice brought her back from her rapt contemplation of his big shoulders and broad chest under the black denim shirt he was wearing—his tattered coat having been discarded before he began his examination of the patients—and she had to blink rapidly before she could say, 'Is feline enteritis bad?' She had never really come into contact with many animals and didn't have a clue as to their ailments.

'The worst.' Dark, glittering eyes looked up and into hers for a moment. 'Even today, with the full range of modern antibiotics, we can do little to fight it once it's got a hold, and if this cat is feral she could have well been suffering from it. As it is…' He paused, then, leaning back from the limp animal, said, 'She seems too docile to be feral. Of course she's exhausted and starving and very young, little more than a kitten herself, but I've known feral cats who would fight with their last breath. It could be the confinement was hard for her and she was virtually starving before

she gave birth, and once the kittens were born and she was
feeding any nourishment would go to her milk, making her
even weaker. I've got a feeling—'

He stopped abruptly, and Candy said, 'What? What is
it?'

He continued somewhat reluctantly, 'I've got an idea she
might have been a domestic pet who got thrown out when
the owners realised she was going to have kittens.'

'Oh, no, surely not?' Candy was horrified. 'People
wouldn't be so cruel.'

'You would be surprised.' It was very grim. 'And, like
I said, she really is very young.'

'She's not going to die?' Candy asked urgently.

'Not if I can help it.' His eyes were narrowed as he
glanced down at the supine animal. 'No, not if I can help
it.'

All his interest and energy was centred on the cat and
her kittens, so how come she was vitally conscious of every
movement, every muscle, every expression of his? Candy
asked herself desperately. She didn't *want* to be; in fact if
she never felt a spark of interest for any man ever again it
would suit her down to the ground, so how come Quinn
Ellington had got under her skin as he had? Mind you, she
had read somewhere ages ago that women were naturally
drawn to doctors and consultants and veterinaries—men
who were powerful in their own field, strong, decisive, but
with the compassionate, protective side their vocations demanded—so it was probably just that. And with his striking
good looks and physical build... Yes, it was that—it wasn't
Quinn as a man, a *person*.

'...help me?'

'Sorry?' She flushed hotly as she realised Quinn had
been speaking and she hadn't heard a word.

'I said I'm going to give her a couple of injections and
then try getting some food down her. Normally I'd sedate

her slightly and put her straight on a drip, but it might make her anxious and it'll be difficult with the kittens. Once I'm satisfied she can travel I'll take her back to the surgery and leave you in peace.'

'Oh, no, no.' And, at his raised eyebrows, 'I mean, I can look after her here. If you think it's possible, of course.'

'I'm not sure. It depends how she responds in the next hour or so,' Quinn said quietly. 'And even if she responds well a cat and kittens is quite a commitment on time and energy. I don't like to see kittens leave Mum until they are about eight weeks old, so you're talking a couple of months of hard work, and then there's the task of finding them all homes—including the female.'

'I know, I know.' She hadn't, but somehow it was suddenly terribly important that she take care of the little family and help them. She couldn't have explained it, even to herself, but she needed to do it. To bring good out of a bad situation. And added to that she had to admit that this solitude wasn't all it was cracked up to be.

She didn't want human companionship—*definitely* not, she told herself vehemently—but animals were different.

The cat took no notice when the needle went in, and soon she was ensconced with the kittens in Essie's oval wicker washing basket on top of Quinn's big thick quilted coat—'It's only an old one I use for work, so they might as well have it,' he'd offered. Quinn made up some of the highly nutritious cat food for feeding mothers and special powdered milk for kittens which he'd had the foresight to bring with him, and managed to get a few spoonfuls of food down her.

Candy fed the kittens, one by one, with the small feeding bottle Quinn had brought, and she had never enjoyed herself so much in all her life. Their tiny, ravishingly beautiful faces and tightly shut eyes were enthralling, and the way they slurped at the bottle was indicative of how hungry they were.

'I think you found them just in time.' Quinn had moved from the other side of the blanket to sit beside her on the rug as she fed the last of the three, his body inclined towards her—which forced Candy to acknowledge her own awareness of him.

She continued to concentrate very hard on the tiny mite in her hands, but he was bent close enough for her to scent his male warmth and it was difficult. Much more difficult than she would have liked.

'They're so sweet.' She had to swallow twice before she could speak, and he obviously noticed and jumped to the conclusion that she was anxious about the cat and her kittens, which she was, she was, she reiterated silently, but that wasn't why she was dry-mouthed and trembly.

'It's easy to say, but try not to worry and think the worst.' The kitten she was holding had had its fill and he gently took it from her, placing it with the others before turning to her again. 'It's so far, so good,' he said quietly, 'okay? And for all Mum's fragility it looks like she's not going to give in, probably because of those little tykes.'

They both looked down at the three tiny kittens, who had squirmed into position and were lying snuggled against their mother.

'Mum's been fed, babies have been fed, and that's all we can do at the moment, but I'll try her with a little more food in half an hour or so. At least with the kittens feeding as they have it means the pressure is off her at the moment, although these dry preparations can't compete with Mum's milk, of course.'

'No, I suppose not.' She suddenly felt as gauche and inadequate as a schoolgirl. The roaring fire, the sleeping family in the wicker basket, the howling of the wind outside and the warmth and cosiness of Essie's little haven—it was too intimate. Far, far too intimate.

Candy rose with an abruptness that startled them both, and because she couldn't think of anything else to say she found herself babbling, 'You must be longing for a drink after all your hard work? What would you like? There's tea or coffee or chocolate, or maybe you'd prefer a glass of wine?'

'A glass of wine would be great,' Quinn said gravely, as though girls reacted to him like cats on a hot tin roof every day. 'As long as you're having one too?'

Oh, yes, she was having one, Candy thought somewhat feverishly. If ever she needed a glass of wine it was right now.

Quinn opened the wine, after she had managed to break the cork in the bottle, and he did it expertly, of course, Candy thought resentfully, as she fetched two large crystal glasses out of the cupboard. But then he would do everything expertly; he was that sort of a man. A continuation along that line was beyond her—he was too close, too big, too *male* to let her imagination have free rein.

'Thank you.' She took the glass of deep, rich red liquid with a tight little smile as she eyed him warily. He was still smeared with blood, and some of those scratches looked nasty; she couldn't let him just slowly fester, could she? 'Look, you need a bath to clean those scratches. Why don't you take your wine up with you while I keep an eye on the invalids?' she said as brightly as she could manage. 'You'll see the clean towels on the shelf at the side of the washbasin.'

'Really? Are you sure?'

His surprise was a reproach. He didn't think she was that mean, did he? Candy asked herself silently. She *had* called him out just before his evening surgery and then forced him to battle with a foe that was all teeth and claws, and she was talking about the hawthorn bush, here, not the felines! She could hardly deny him a bath, especially when he seemed agreeable to hanging about and seeing if the cat could recover enough to stay here rather than being carted off to the clinical surroundings of the veterinary practice.

'Of course.' Her tone was airy, as though she offered hundreds of men the same privilege.

'Thank you.' His voice was soft and low and kind of smoky, and it made Candy shiver. And regret the offer. Quinn Ellington naked in her bathroom... What was she doing playing with fire?

He was downstairs again in twenty minutes, barefoot, his black hair still damp and his denim shirt open at the neck and showing a smidgen of soft, silky body hair. He was one sexy customer. She busied herself with the cat food and only turned at the last moment to say, 'Do you think she might eat it herself this time? She had a drop of milk while you were upstairs.'

'Did she? That's good, very good.' He was all professionalism as he squatted on his heels at the side of the basket, and Candy berated herself for her carnal thoughts. But his black jeans *were* blatantly tight across the hips, she comforted herself in the next moment, and she couldn't help having eyes, could she?

The cat roused herself enough to take an interest in the food Candy offered this time, managing half a saucer before she sank back into the folds of Quinn's coat, the kittens squeaking and mewing at the movement.

'I think we're winning.'

You might be, but I'm beginning to wonder, Candy thought ruefully, as Quinn slanted a satisfied smile at her. There were good-looking men and there were sexy men, and then there was Quinn Ellington.

'Mind if I take a look?' He had risen to his feet and sauntered over to her easel, standing under the window. As was normal when she'd finished for the day she had thrown a cover over the painting, and now Candy hesitated before shrugging slowly.

'I won't if you'd rather I didn't.' His hand had stayed on the cover and he sounded quite unperturbed. It would have been the easiest thing in the world to make some excuse, but somehow, and she didn't know why, Candy found herself saying, 'I don't mind, but don't expect Rembrandt.'

'I rarely expect anything from anyone,' Quinn said dryly.

'Oh.' She didn't know quite how to take that, but there had been a darkness in the words that hadn't been there in their earlier conversation.

She joined him at the easel, removing the cover herself and watching his face as she did so. As Quinn let his narrowed eyes wander over the painting she could read nothing in his dark countenance to suggest what he was thinking. And then he said, his eyes still on the silver crystal-bright scene, 'This is quite exquisite, Candy. Outstanding, in fact. I had no idea…'

She blushed bright pink; she couldn't help it. The admiration and respect were so genuine she couldn't doubt he meant every word. 'Thank you.'

'If this is indicative of your work you are going to be a force to be reckoned with in the art world,' he continued quietly, still examining the picture before turning the ebony gaze on her flushed face and adding, 'Has your agent confirmed about the exhibition in London yet?'

She hadn't expected him to remember, and now her cheeks matched her poppy-red cashmere jumper. 'Not yet, but he seems to think it might happen in late spring.'

Quinn nodded slowly. 'So, something to aim for?'

It was a question, not a statement, and she stared at him for some moments. He saw too much, this man. 'Yes.' It was short and cryptic.

'That wasn't a criticism, Candy. Everyone has to have something to aim for. There was a time in my life when my career became my salvation.' He had felt her tension slam the door shut, although he didn't betray it, his tone easy and casual.

'And now?'

'Now?' Quinn looked down at his bare feet for a moment, considering his answer as he raked back that errant lock of hair from his forehead.

He still hadn't had a haircut, Candy thought, but he was one of the few men she had come across who could wear his hair over-long and look even more masculine if anything.

'Now it's my life,' he said simply, raising his eyes to take hers, 'and I like it that way.'

What was he saying exactly? Candy stared at him, conscious of the fact that she couldn't very well ask him the sort of leading personal questions she would like to when she wouldn't afford Quinn the same privilege. He obviously wasn't going to say any more and so she nodded dismissively, her voice flat as she said, 'That's exactly how I feel; my career is my life. I want to succeed and that takes dedication and effort.'

'It appears we're kindred spirits,' he observed with a lazy smile that made Candy's heart beat a little faster, 'so how about burying the hatchet and being friends as well? Ready to start again?'

'What?' She was honestly bewildered at the turnabout in conversation.

'We got off on the wrong foot,' Quinn said pleasantly, 'and I take full blame for that. You had the idea I was going to hover over you like a guardian angel and report back to Essie and Xavier, right?'

'I…' It was exactly what she had thought.

'And maybe there was an element of something like that

in my thinking before I met you.' He raised dark eyebrows. 'But believe me, Candy, I realised my mistake very quickly. You are quite capable of looking after yourself, as you've made very clear.'

The dry note in his voice was very distinct, but this time Candy refused to blush.

'It seems ridiculous that with you knowing few people at present and our mutual connections we can't be on good terms. Agreed?'

Candy looked at him blankly as her mind raced at express speed. There were no doubt thousands, millions of men and women who managed to have perfectly platonic friendships with members of the opposite sex. And if it had been nice little Jamie in front of her—whom she'd met briefly at Essie's wedding—she would probably be agreeing enthusiastically to what had just been voiced. But it wasn't the freckle-faced, ginger-haired Jamie gazing down at her. It was Quinn. And Quinn was... Well, he wasn't five-foot-eight with freckles and a snub nose.

He was disturbing. Disturbing and intimidating and aggressively male, and he made her feel uncomfortable and on edge and a hundred other things besides, none of which were welcome.

He, on the other hand, clearly had no problem at all in viewing her in the same way he would a chum at the rugby club or something similar!

But this was her problem, not his. The innate honesty that was an integral part of Candy's make-up forced her to face the truth. He had offered the olive branch and in the circumstances she could do little else than receive it with both hands. The man had rushed to her rescue—or more precisely to the cat and kittens' rescue—and hadn't put a foot wrong from the first time she had met him, if she analysed it. It had been her that had been prickly and difficult. All he had done was to make the cottage comfortable for her, stock up her cupboards and generally behave like the proverbial good neigbour!

Candy took a deep breath, smiled sweetly and said, 'I'd be pleased to count you as one of my friends, Quinn.'

'Great.' He stood looking down at her with glittering black eyes. 'And do friends run to a couple of slices of buttered toast, maybe?'

'Oh, I'm sorry.' She belatedly realised it was now well past teatime. 'I can do better than toast, if you like? Spaghetti bolognese, or perhaps you'd prefer pork chops?'

'Spaghetti, definitely.'

He grinned at her, and she valiantly ignored what it did to her nerve-endings.

Quinn perched on one of the stools at the tiny breakfast bar while Candy prepared the bolognese sauce, and once she had added a pinch of grated nutmeg and the cinnamon and oregano to the minced beef, onions, tomatoes and tomato purée, all simmering gently in their wine and stock base, he poured them another glass of wine.

'My spaghetti bolognese comes out of a jar.'

His eyes smiled at her as he spoke, and she was extremely pleased at the casual smile she managed in return. 'Xavier's old housekeeper, Mrs Martella, was Italian, and when I was growing up she used to teach me all kinds of dishes. She was a fantastic cook, but she'd never allow a tin or jar of anything in her kitchen; she was fanatical about it. I do cheat sometimes, but I have to admit Mrs Martella's way tastes better.'

'It certainly smells delicious.'

Candy popped the lid on the pan and took a sip of her drink as she looked at him out of the corner of her eye. 'So you're not one of these men who's a wow in the kitchen?' she asked carefully, telling herself she was just making conversation rather than trying to find out more about him.

'I can just about boil an egg,' he admitted ruefully. 'My father is the same. I used to think it was because my mother is the sort of old-fashioned housewife who won't let a man into the kitchen, but when I went to university I discovered I had a natural gift for causing havoc anywhere near a stove. I drop things, I burn things, and I can *never* get everything to finish cooking at the same time.'

Did he know how attractive that air of little-boy-lost was when combined with his particular brand of dark, vigorous maleness? Candy thought suspiciously. She took another sip of her wine and waved an arm towards the fire. 'This will take about thirty-five or forty minutes now, so we might as well be comfortable,' she said quietly, making sure that once she was across the other side of the room she made for one of the chairs and left the sofa to Quinn.

However, he chose to drop down on the floor, sitting at the side of the flickering fire close to his sleeping feline patients, one knee drawn up and the other leg straight, his back resting against the wall next to the mantelpiece. It was a casual pose, the pose of a man totally at ease with himself and his surroundings, and perversely Candy felt irritated as she glanced his way from her vantage point of the chair opposite.

How could he be so completely relaxed? So unaware of this—this *electricity* in the air? she asked herself testily. But she clearly didn't do a thing for him. And that was good—very, very, good, she assured herself silently. It *was*. It was certainly the only way any contact between them could work.

'So, if you can't cook how do you manage most days?' she asked, after a few moments when his disturbing presence had got her to the point of speaking or screaming. 'Microwave? Ready meals?'

'Mostly.' His head had been back and his eyes shut, which had accentuated his brooding quality of toughness tenfold, but now he glanced at her and nodded. 'And Marion has taken me under her wing, which helps. Home-made fruit cakes, scones, pot roasts, egg custards—I get the lot, bless her. She fusses a bit, but she's got a heart of gold.'

'I'm surprised she hasn't had a try at matchmaking,' Candy said with a wry smile. 'Isn't that what mumsy women do in her position?'

'Don't.' Quinn grimaced. 'I've already had the virtues of her daughter held up before me on more than one occasion, and she apparently has a younger sister in town who's fancy-free too.'

'Oh, dear.' She eyed him over the top of her glass. 'And you didn't avail yourself of either lady?'

He shrugged. 'I prefer to arrange my own dates.' It was dismissive, and stated this particular line in conversation was finished, but Candy suddenly felt stubborn.

'You might have met the woman of your dreams.'

'I doubt it.' This time his tone was even more cryptic.

'How do you know until you give them a try? There might be a Mrs Ellington hiding out there,' she said with a light smile.

'No way. Marriage is not on my agenda,' he said shortly.

'How can you say that until you've tried it?' she argued quietly, not really knowing why she was pursuing this but unable to stop.

'I can say it because I have tried it, Candy,' he said grimly, rising to his feet and placing the half-full glass of wine on the mantelpiece as he spoke. 'And it looks like Mum is ready for some more food. I'll see to her while you check the dinner, shall I?'

He had padded across to the breakfast bar for the cat food in the next moment, but Candy sat quite still for a full five seconds more. He had put her in her place and he'd had every right to do so; she'd been unforgivably nosy and she knew it. But *married*? He had been married?

Ridiculous, but she felt as bad as if someone had just bopped her right on the chin.

CHAPTER THREE

CONTRARY to what Candy had thought in the first embarrassing and highly charged minutes after Quinn's revelation, the rest of the evening went relatively smoothly.

The spaghetti bolognese was wonderful, and Quinn was highly appreciative; they fed the kittens again and the mother cat ate more food and drank a saucer full of creamy milk—and Quinn kept the conversation light and easy. Her work, his work; the advantages and pitfalls of small-town life; art and books… All safe, fairly innocuous subjects. He was amusing and funny and entertaining and the time just flew, and when—at just gone eleven—he decided that the cat and her kittens could stay with Candy for the night at least, she was amazed that it was so late.

When she opened the front door for him to leave they saw it had stopped snowing and the white glistening world outside the cottage was breathtakingly silent. The moon was shedding a thin hollow light into the darkness, turning the frost lying like crystals on the snow to a carpet of diamond dust. It was cold, bitterly cold, and as Quinn stepped out into the garden Candy shivered.

'Don't catch cold.' He took her hand as he spoke, leaning forward and brushing her cheek with the lightest of gossamer kisses as he said, 'Thanks for the dinner, Candy; I haven't enjoyed myself so much in ages.'

It was a social kiss, the kiss of a friend, and despite her pounding heart she said steadily, 'Thank *you* for coming to our rescue,' and ignored what the smell and feel of him had done to her nerve-endings.

'My pleasure.' Quinn didn't want a relationship, and he

knew the tall, slim redhead in front of him wanted one even less. So why, knowing that, was he finding it difficult to leave? he asked himself silently. Why did he want to take her in his arms properly and kiss her until they both went up in flames and he was back in the cottage and up the stairs and in her bed? 'I'll call you in the morning and see how they are.' He indicated towards the wicker basket behind Candy with an inclination of his head.

'I think they are going to be fine.'

That accent of hers, the soft, slow, easy drawl, was incredibly sexy. *She* was incredibly sexy. All glowing tumbled hair and big bright wide eyes. But he wasn't in the market for sexy redheads, or not this one anyway. Candy was Xavier's niece and Essie had cast him in the role of protector, which was fair enough. And he would fulfil that role to the best of his ability. No problem.

'I think so too, but that presents its own set of problems,' Quinn said steadily. 'For a start the cat might have got lost and have an anxious owner looking for it. And, like I said, a cat and kittens are expensive both in terms of time and money.'

'Do you think that? That she might have an owner who is looking for her?' Candy asked anxiously.

'Would that be so bad?'

'Yes.' It was immediate, and although he had sensed that would be her answer he inwardly groaned. She'd fallen in love with the little family. She was too tender-hearted and compassionate by half, the sort of person the world delighted in kicking in the teeth.

Immediately the thought hit he didn't like it. He knew nothing about Candy Grey and furthermore he didn't want to know anything, besides which he, of all people, knew that the female sex were experts in projecting the image they wanted you to see. She might be as hardboiled as they come under that marshmallow softness.

Although he knew that wasn't the case.

Again he refuted his gut instinct and said instead, his ebony eyes unreadable and his voice cool, 'You have to face the fact there might be an owner out there who wants her back, Candy. And what are you going to do with a cat and three kittens anyway?'

'Look after them, love them.'

Hell. He nodded abruptly. 'Well, we'll see. Don't worry about it for now, and, like I said, I'll give you a call in the morning.'

'All right.'

It was disconsolate, and again he had to resist the impulse to take her into his arms. He wasn't sure what he was feeling, but as his heart began to hammer in his ribcage it was a warning to leave.

'Goodnight, Candy.'

This time he turned and made his way towards the gate through the snow, which was inches thick, and it wasn't until he was seated in the Landrover Discovery that he glanced back towards the lighted doorway. She was still standing there, the light behind her silhouetting her slim shape in the bright red sweater and black leggings she was wearing.

He started the engine, raised a hand briefly and backed the big vehicle carefully past Candy's car and out into the lane. And then he drove away without looking towards the cottage again.

As the vehicle ploughed up the narrow track Quinn found his thoughts were going round and round in his head. He didn't like the emotions that had besieged him throughout the night. For the last three years he had kept both his thoughts and his feelings under firm control and that was the way it was going to stay, he told himself grimly as his eyes hardened.

He had had enough of bowel-twisting emotion to last

him a lifetime, more than enough. Never again would a woman do to him what Laura had done. He breathed deeply through his nose, refusing to allow the memories he kept behind the closed door of his mind to break out.

He was satisfied with his life. He had his own successful practice which was growing daily; he would soon need to employ another veterinary and perhaps another nurse to assist on a part-time basis. The flat above the surgery was very much a bachelor pad but more than suited his needs; he had had to change very little of the decor or furnishings Xavier had bought and sold along with the business. He dated when it suited him—casual, no-strings-attached affairs, where each party knew the score and acted accordingly. He operated on the powers of reason and logic. He had been a blind fool once but he would never make the same mistake again.

It was friendship he had offered Candy and it was friendship she had accepted, and if ever he felt it was bordering on something else... It would be dealt with, and ruthlessly.

He reached the top of the lane and nosed the four-by-four carefully into the main road, straightened his shoulders, raked back his hair and put all further thoughts of Candy Grey out of his mind.

Candy fed the cat twice more during the night, and by the time Quinn telephoned just after ten the kittens were feeding from their mother and everything in the house was hunky-dory. Almost.

If she had allowed her mind to linger on the uneasy feeling in the pit of her stomach it would have told her the deep-seated agitation was less to do with the fact that there might be an anxious owner waiting to claim the cat and more to do with a certain ebony-eyed vet. But she didn't dwell on her misgivings over the wisdom of elevating Quinn to the position of friend beyond reassuring herself, several times, that she was perfectly in control of all the circumstances in her life at present, beyond that of the felines' ultimate home.

'Candy?' Quinn's voice was cool and calm, even remote. He was obviously in work mode, she thought, and this was a duty call because he had promised. 'How are things?'

Things? she thought a trifle feverishly, before swallowing hard and saying, with studied nonchalance, 'Absolutely fine, Quinn. The kittens are feeding well and Tabitha is eating like a horse. She's been out once, but came straight back to the kittens.'

'Tabitha?'

'The cat. I couldn't just keep calling her Cat or Mother or whatever,' Candy said defensively.

'No, I guess not. Look, I've made a few enquiries, and as far as I can ascertain no one for miles around seems to be missing a tortoiseshell female, but that's not to say you're home and dry,' he added warningly.

'But it's hopeful?'

'Yes, I'd say it's hopeful,' he agreed shortly. 'I'm sending Philippa, my nurse, down later, with a few bits and pieces you'll need, so if there's any supplies for yourself you're short of...?'

'Oh, I can manage, really. I've got the car,' she said hastily.

'You won't get up the lane in that; it was pretty snowbound last night. I'll get her to bring you a loaf, milk, things like that, okay? Look, I must go; we're pretty busy today. Ring me if you're worried about the cat or kittens, won't you?'

'Yes, thank you.'

She was surprised at the flat feeling that assailed her when she put the receiver down, but put it down to anti-climax regarding her worry about what the results of Quinn's investigations might have found. But it looked as if everything was okay. She stared across at Tabitha, who stared back with great smoky-green eyes and then yawned widely, showing sharp little white teeth. 'He's sending his nurse,' she told the watching feline. 'He's too busy to come himself.' Which was fine. Absolutely no problem. It was good of him to offer to do that, wasn't it? Very good.

Philippa arrived at midday and she was very nice, bustling in with bags of groceries before returning to the Discovery and bringing more cat food, a large bag of cat litter and a tray, a couple of pottery feeding bowls and a big thick blanket she said she'd found in the back of one of the cupboards at the practice, and several other things besides.

She was also a sweet-faced, blue-eyed blonde, with an hourglass figure, a skin like peaches and cream and the sort of wide-eyed, innocent appeal that would turn on any red-blooded male under the age of eighty.

Candy made them both a cup of coffee, listened to Philippa enthuse first about Tabitha and the kittens and then about how *lucky* she was to be working for such a brilliant vet and fabulous person as Quinn, and how she just adored *everything* about her job, and then waved her goodbye some thirty minutes later, by which time all the eager, fervent exuberance had made Candy feel as old as Methuselah.

Had she ever been as young and carefree as that girl? she asked herself as she plumped down beside the basket and stroked Tabitha, who greeted her reappearance with a satisfied purr. She didn't think so. The circumstances of her birth, her grandmother dying and Xavier becoming her sole guardian and all the family she had when she was eight had made her a solemn little girl and a wary teenager.

The only time she had blossomed had been when she'd met Harper. Suddenly her fiancé's face was there in her thoughts, and whether it was lack of sleep or all the emotional turmoil involving the cat she wasn't sure, but she found she couldn't keep the memories under lock and key as she usually could.

She had loved him so much and been so happy. She bit her lip hard and glanced down at the tiny kittens—the two little females carbon copies of their beautiful mother and the other, according to Quinn, who had determined their sex the night before, a jet-black little tom—as she sighed deeply.

If they had crashed the night before the accident she would never have known about Ellie-Sue. Ellie-Sue, the waitress at the local fast-food restaurant whom Harper had been playing around with for months and who had decided Harper was the father of her unborn child. He had told her over a candlelit dinner at an expensive restaurant, stating that Ellie-Sue meant absolutely nothing to him and that he loved her, Candy, and had seemed almost surprised when she had stormed out of the building to the car.

They had rowed bitterly on the way home. When he had realised she was serious about finishing the engagement he had turned ugly, telling her it was all her fault, that if she hadn't been frigid he wouldn't have had to satisfy himself elsewhere and that Xavier could easily afford to pay Ellie-Sue enough to keep her quiet.

As it was the girl had married some other guy just three weeks after Harper's funeral, so it looked as though Ellie-Sue had had more than one beau on the go at the same time... Candy rose abruptly, walking across to her painting and jerking off the cover with a trembling hand.

Harper had been marrying her because she was the niece—virtually the beloved daughter—of a millionaire, as much as anything else. He had seen her as a meal ticket. An attractive, pleasant meal ticket, but a meal ticket none the less. And she hadn't guessed. She hadn't had so much as the whiff of an inkling before that terrible night. That was what had haunted her—frightened her to death in the aftermath of the accident. It had shaken her to the core of her being that she could have got it so wrong, and her faith in herself had been shattered.

Harper had made her feel she was nothing, less than nothing. A nonentity. And it had been a hard, slow climb out of the despair and pain as she had gradually clawed back a measure of self-confidence. But she still didn't trust her own judgement or discernment; perhaps she never would. One thing she *did* know. She would never put herself in such a vulnerable position again.

She didn't want to fall in love. She didn't want to experience the highs and the lows, the ecstasy and the agony. She was finished with all that. She couldn't go through what she had just come out of again and remain sane.

But she didn't have to.

She stood gazing at the painting without really seeing it. She was well again. That was a priceless gift in itself. She could make her own future on her own terms and if nothing else the near death experience she had gone through had enhanced even the most ordinary day-to-day aspects of living. She had always been particularly aware of and sensitive to beauty, but now her senses had been sharpened to a point that was almost painful. And that could only improve her painting.

She had lost something but she had been given something back in return. The possibility of marriage, motherhood, all the things that had once been so important, was gone, but she would carve a career that was spectacular. She *would*. Her soft mouth drooped unknowingly, but then her eyes focused on the painting and her back straightened. Time to get to work.

*   *   *

Over the next three weeks the snow melted, hard white frosts replaced the slush and mud, and December dawned bright but bitterly cold.

Quinn had telephoned Candy every two or three days for an update on the cat and kittens but he hadn't visited, and so when on the first Friday in December she heard the sound of the four-by-four outside she immediately glanced at Tabitha, suspecting the worst. He had found her owner! Oh, she wouldn't be able to bear it.

The cat stared back serenely before cuffing an errant kitten as it attempted to scramble up the first tread of the stairs. It was the black one, of course, Alfie. Although only three weeks old, he was into everything, unlike his demure sisters, but he was bold and cheeky and Candy loved him.

Her heart lurched when she opened the front door and saw Quinn approaching, and it wasn't altogether due to apprehension regarding the cat.

'Hi.' She managed a fairly steady smile. He had had a haircut and he took her breath away.

'Hi, yourself.' He grinned easily and then, as Tabitha shot past Candy to wrap herself voluptuously round his legs, they both looked down at the little cat in surprise.

'She remembers you.' Still, what female wouldn't?

'Hallo, puss.' He bent down and stroked the sleek fur which felt like silk before straightening again and walking, with Tabitha weaving in and out of his legs with amazing dexterity, to stand in front of her.

'Before I offer you a coffee, this isn't to say you've found her owner, is it?' Candy asked with careful control.

'What?' And then, as he realised, 'No, no, of course not. Hell, is that what you thought? I'm sorry, Candy. No, this is to ask you a favour, actually.'

'Right.' The relief was overwhelming.

Once inside the warmth and brightness of the cottage Quinn bent down and scooped Alfie up into one large hand as the kitten attempted a kamikaze dive through the front door just as Candy went to close it behind them.

'Nimble little fellow, isn't he?'

The tender amusement with which he spoke about the kitten brought all sorts of feelings to the fore, and none of them were helpful. Candy looked into the hard, handsome face and reminded herself he wasn't here to see *her*, Candy Grey. He was here to ask a favour; he'd said so.

'I'll put the coffee on,' she said evenly.

Quinn nodded, glancing down at Tabitha and her two daughters, who were sitting prettily beside their mother. 'I'll just have a look at this lot while you do that and then we can have a chat,' he said nonchalantly.

'Fine.'

She watched him from the kitchen as he examined each small feline and their mother, and by the time she poured the coffee Quinn had pronounced them all well and thriving.

'When are you going to start looking for homes for them?' he asked as he came to join her at the breakfast bar and she passed him his coffee and a plate of chocolate-chip cookies.

'I'm not.' The dark eyebrows raised themselves, and in answer to them she said, 'Tabitha deserves to keep them all after what she went through, and this place is perfect for animals. I'll come to you soon to get the kittens vaccinated, and perhaps we'd better make sure Tabitha doesn't get romanced again, but I like the idea of having them around.'

'They could prove expensive.'

She shrugged. 'I can manage.'

'And what about when you go home to Canada?'

Candy's stomach contracted, and it was only in that moment she realised she was planning to stay in England for some time. 'I'll take them with me if I go,' she said quietly, 'but I like it here. I might be staying for quite a while.'

'You'll get homesick after a few months,' Quinn said expressionlessly.

She raised her chin slightly. It almost sounded as though he *wanted* her to go, she thought grimly. 'I don't think so.'

'Well, you're the best judge of that.' It was dispassionate and detached.

Yes, she was, she thought militantly, taking a gulp of the scalding hot coffee and then trying not to choke as it burnt her throat and made her eyes water. And it was nothing to do with Quinn one way or the other either, irritating man that he was!

Quinn munched his way through the plate of rich, crumbly cookies with a dedication that left no time for conversation, and when the last morsel had gone he put down his coffee mug, his expression unreadable. 'I expect you're wondering why I called,' he said quietly.

Candy shrugged elegantly. After that remark about her returning to Canada she was proffering nothing, she told herself tightly. She could match him for cool remoteness any day. 'Not particularly,' she drawled blandly. 'I was used to friends dropping by all the time back home.' Put that in your pipe and smoke it, Quinn Ellington! And she didn't care a jot about Philippa!

He nodded, his hand lifting to rake back his hair and then pausing halfway. The new shorn style of the raven-black crop wouldn't move in a hurricane. 'I got it cut,' he said in explanation. 'I keep forgetting.'

She inclined her head, allowing a slight smile to touch her lips. 'It suits you.'

'Yeah, well, I told them I probably wouldn't be back for another six months so they needed to do a hatchet job.'

He was uncomfortable, if not embarrassed by the compliment, Candy realised in amazement. He was easily the most devastatingly attractive man for miles around and he was actually embarrassed because she had said she liked his haircut.

It was at that moment an unexpected quiver ran through her, a subtle stirring of her blood that made her tingle in all her intimate places. She lowered her eyes to her coffee mug and drained it before saying briskly, 'Another coffee?'

'Thanks.'

He had settled back on his stool, perched on the other side of the breakfast bar, after pushing his empty mug towards her, and he actually cleared his throat before saying, 'The thing is, Candy, I need a favour.'

'Yes?' She poured two more coffees, pushed his towards him, but remained where she was in the kitchen. 'What can I do for you?'

What could she do for him? Quinn's eyes were inscrutable as he stared into the lovely face opposite him. She looked about sixteen this morning, with that glorious hair tied back in a high shining ponytail and her beautiful face scrubbed clean of make-up, but there was nothing adolescent about that luscious figure. She was one hell of a woman.

A muscle worked in his jaw. And maybe this wasn't such a good idea? But it was too late now; he'd said too much. His thoughts caused his voice to be abrupt as he said, 'I need you to pretend to be my girlfriend for the evening.'

Her eyes widened; her mouth partly opened. Whatever she had imagined it wasn't this. 'You need...'

'Look, let me explain.' His hand went to his hair again and then he gave an impatient click of his teeth. 'This is a relatively small town, and the social scene isn't the hottest in the world, but as the resident vet I get invited to quite a few parties and dinners, that sort of thing. And as a bachelor I always seem to be the target for predatory females, or worse—predatory mothers with daughters they are desperate to offload. Get the picture?'

She nodded even as she thought, It's not because he's a bachelor, or not *just* that anyway. Quinn would always draw women—predatory or otherwise.

'Don't get me wrong, I'm more than able to fend off any attacks,' he said with wry humour, 'and I've always made it clear I'm not the marrying kind. However, there's one lady who is more persistent than most and it's got kind of embarrassing. You aren't interested in any kind of permanent relationship at the moment, right?'

She nodded somewhat dazedly.

'And we're friends. Right again?' he said persuasively.

Oh, no, no, he wasn't going to use that to manoeuvre her into a corner, was he? It appeared he was.

'So…'

'So?'

'So you don't know anyone here yet; there's no bosom friend to know you'd be acting a part and it would be the easiest thing in the world to help me out.' He eyed her wary face. 'I'd do the same for you,' he added compellingly.

He might do. He very well might do. But whereas she obviously left him stone-cold, he didn't have the same effect on *her* hormones, Candy told herself crossly.

'And it'd be a great way for you to meet some of the locals. All work and no play…'

She stared at him. 'What, exactly, would this play-acting involve, Quinn?' she asked directly.

Good question. In the intervening weeks since he had last seen her he had forgotten—or perhaps he should say he had tried to forget—just how beautiful she was. 'Exactly what you want it to,' he said evenly.

Ball back in her court again. She took a big gulp of coffee, glanced towards the window, and then at Tabitha, who appeared to be listening intently to all that was being said from her vantage point at the entrance into the kitchen area and was ignoring her charges for once, and tried desperately to sort out the wheat from the chaff.

The last thing she wanted was a romantic involvement of any kind, but Quinn was totally in agreement on that score. He had been nothing but kindness since she'd arrived, and just great over the affair with Tabitha and the kittens. She did owe him. And if she was totally honest she *had* been getting a little bored the last week or two. She loved the cottage and this life, she qualified hastily, she really did, but a little social intercourse wouldn't come amiss. And in her role of Quinn's girlfriend she wouldn't have to worry about any man getting the wrong impression.

She could enjoy herself, meet all the local folk and relax knowing they knew she was already 'spoken for'. Everything to gain and nothing to lose. She wasn't cut out to be a total hermit. The thought brought a silent smile to her lips. She was still smiling as her eyes focused on Quinn's dark face again, and she said, her voice quiet but steady, 'Of course if I can help out at all I'd be happy to, Quinn, and it would be nice to meet your friends and acquaintances.'

'Excellent.'

Excellent, he'd said. So why, in the last minute or two, did he feel as though he had made a mistake? Quinn asked himself silently. He had been quite truthful regarding Joanna Embleton-White. The woman had become a perfect menace, following him about and even cornering him at Colonel Llewellyn's party the week before. She was shameless. But it wasn't Joanna who had prompted the suggestion that Candy accompany him to Meg Andrews' dinner; it was more his promise to Essie that he would try and draw Candy into the social scene as soon as he could. Essie had been worried Candy would shut herself away.

And that was the only reason? His promise to Essie? The snide little voice at the back of his mind was challenging. He hadn't used the promise as a means to an end because he wanted to be with Candy? it asked baldly. Come on, who was he trying to fool?

'Where is this...?'

'Dinner. It's a dinner,' Quinn said quickly, 'at Meg Andrews' house. She's a solicitor, and one of the local big fish in this particular little pool, but a very nice lady for all that. You'll like her. I'll pick you up next Saturday evening at round about eight, if that suits?'

'Fine.' Candy finished her coffee. 'Formal dress?'

Quinn nodded. 'Meg likes to dress up,' he said, a trifle apologetically.

'Okay.' It was dismissive, and as Candy's gaze wandered across the room towards the easel Quinn stood up. She clearly wanted him to leave, he thought, and he was surprised and not a little disturbed that he felt put out.

'Till Saturday, then.' His voice was cool and he was already walking towards the door as he said over his shoulder, 'Thanks for the coffee.'

Candy didn't follow him immediately to the door, but by the time Quinn had reached the Discovery she was standing in the doorway and raised a hand in a brief goodbye.

Those last few minutes, as the enormity of what she had promised had washed over her, had been difficult. As the tail-lights disappeared up the lane she raised both hands to her hot cheeks. She was going out on a date with Quinn Ellington!

Well, okay, perhaps not a date in the true sense of the word, she amended silently, but nevertheless she was already regretting the impulse that had led her to say yes. She stared out over the white garden which, despite the fact that it was mid-morning, was still held firm in the grip of a hard, sparkling frost.

Oh, well, she'd done it now. Tabitha appeared at her ankles, winding sensuously round her legs and purring like a small train, causing Candy to turn and automatically check where Alfie was.

The small black pom-pom of fur was wobbling across the floor towards her, his two sisters just behind him, and suddenly Candy felt better.

She *did* owe Quinn; he'd been absolutely marvellous when she'd needed him, and it wasn't his fault he was so darn attractive, she told herself firmly. Okay, so she fancied him physically—she might as well face that one and bring it into the light and get it out of the way. But he was very fanciable. She would have had to be six foot under or of a different sexual persuasion not to notice that! And at least it showed she was feeling something again—there had been a time in her depression when she could have had Brad Pitt or Mel Gibson in front of her and not felt a thing.

Quinn wasn't interested in love or commitment and neither was she. He was a career man and she had decided her work was going to be her life, certainly for the next decade or so at least. But her nature didn't naturally lend itself to a solitary existence. It would be nice to meet a few people, and even nicer to have an escort...

She shut the door just as the determined Alfie reached the threshold, and then giggled as the tiny kitten stared up at her reproachfully, his little head on one side as though to say, All that effort and then you spoil it!

Whatever else, this suggestion of Quinn's seemed to indicate he wasn't interested in the lovely Philippa. Perhaps he didn't believe in mixing work and pleasure? Maybe she had a boyfriend? Or it could be—Candy stopped abruptly. Stop it, she warned herself steadily. It's nothing to do with you whether Quinn likes her or not. What on earth was the matter with her, thinking like this?

She would dress up on Saturday, and make sure Quinn didn't regret asking her to masquerade as his girlfriend, but it would be her way of thanking him for all he had done and nothing else. And, who knows, it might be fun?

And then, as though someone had just queried the last statement, Candy said out loud, 'It might—it *might* be fun,' and went back to her painting.

CHAPTER FOUR

THE YEARS of acting as Xavier's hostess for his house parties in Canada meant Candy was not fazed by any sort of social event. She could do the necessary patter, smile sweetly when she was bored stiff and her feet were aching, and converse as easily and warmly with a shy, gauche teenager as a formidable matron of advanced years or a lecherous old goat of a husband.

For the last three or four years in Canada her success at her painting had meant her income was very healthy, and as she had continued to work from home, and had run Xavier's household for him until he had married Essie, she had bought herself an extensive and expensive wardrobe.

Saturday morning saw her selecting and discarding one dress after another in a way she hadn't done for years.

She was nervous, she realised with something of a shock. Nervous that she wouldn't be wearing the right sort of thing, that she wouldn't fit in, that Quinn would be disappointed by her.

'Oh, for goodness' sake pull yourself together, girl!' She glared at her reflection in the mirror as she stood shivering in her silk slip. The downstairs of the cottage was as warm as toast, with the fire blazing and Tabitha and the kittens stretched out in the wicker basket fast asleep, but the upstairs—although not freezing—never got really warm.

'Right, decision time.' Her eyes narrowed and she reached for a sleeveless black crêpe dress with an asymmetric lace border and thin straps, teaming it with precariously high strappy black sandals. The original little black dress. Her nose wrinkled. But she always looked good in black, it suited her colouring, and if she put her hair up and wore the matching gold earrings and necklace Essie and Xavier had bought her the Christmas before she would do.

She laid the dress and matching underwear out on the bed, pulled on jeans and a thick jumper and put all further thoughts of the evening out of her mind. She intended to work today until four o'clock, then have a bath and generally pamper and preen herself, and then... Prepare to be impressed, Quinn Ellington, she warned him silently.

Candy didn't question why she felt the need to impress him as she scurried downstairs and made herself a mug of strong black coffee before starting work. And it was just as well she didn't question herself; it might have spoilt her enjoyment in the day's painting. But at ten to eight that evening, as she heard the Aston Martin in the lane outside the cottage, her stomach was fluttering like a host of butterflies.

And the butterflies went berserk when she opened the door to Quinn. He was in black dinner jacket and tie—immaculate from the top of his raven head to the soles of his shining shoes—and he was the stuff fantasies were made of.

Candy couldn't have spoken to save her life, but she did manage a fairly natural smile as she stood aside and waved her hand for him to enter.

Although he didn't. He kissed her instead. And it was a slow kiss, a pleasurable kiss, a kiss that made her toes curl in the expensive sandals and her cheeks flush. Apart from his lips on hers he wasn't touching her, he hadn't taken her into his arms or made any attempt to move close, but then, as the kiss ended and he stepped into the cottage, he turned and lifted her chin to meet his glittering eyes. 'Canada's loss is England's gain,' he said softly. 'You look fantastic.'

'Thank you.' He had thrown her, completely and utterly thrown her, and because she wasn't thinking straight she said shakily, 'I thought... Friends? I thought we were friends?'

'We are.' This Quinn was new to her, and as unlike the dedicated caring vet or remote, cool ally of Essie as it was possible to be. He was dashingly suave, the smooth and confident Casanova and Lothario, and Candy found herself thinking that if this was the persona he adopted out of working hours he couldn't very well blame these women who made a habit of throwing themselves at him. He asked for it!

'Right.' Her stomach curled over but she couldn't help it; he was so darn *handsome*. 'You usually kiss your friends like that?' she asked with an amused casualness she was inordinately proud of.

'Only the female variety.'

This evening was not such a good idea. If he carried on like this she was going to spoil all his plans by leaping on him herself! The thought was enough to cause her back to straighten and her smile to have an edge to it as she said, 'Perhaps it might be better to save such little touches until there's an audience to appreciate them?'

His eyebrows raised, and then he gave an amused chuckle as he nodded easily. 'Blame it on that dress,' he drawled lazily. 'Like I said, you look fantastic. Here—' he handed her a little box '—although it can't compete with your beauty,' he added gallantly as she opened the lid to see the exquisite rose-tinted orchid nestling on a bed of silk.

'It's beautiful, Quinn. Thank you,' she murmured softly.

'Here, let me.'

He took the flower from her as she lifted it out of the box, pinning it on her dress with an expertise that told Candy he had done the same thing many times before. To many women. But she knew he had had women, lots of women, she told herself tightly as her heart jumped at the thought. He must be thirty-three, thirty-four maybe, and you didn't get to that age—looking like Quinn—without being sexually experienced. And he'd been married. She mustn't forget that, she warned herself shakily as she made every effort to ignore the feel of his warm, firm fingers on the soft flesh of her upper breasts as he fixed the orchid in place.

'Shall we go?' She took a step backwards away from him as she spoke, reaching for her wrap which was hanging over the back of the chair and checking the guard was fixed firmly round the fire. Alfie was too inquisitive by half, and although the little family were fast asleep at the moment she didn't trust the black kitten.

The night was cold and crisp as they stepped out of the warmth of the cottage, but the severe frosts of the last few days had given way to slightly milder weather. Nevertheless, Candy shivered as they walked down the path towards the Aston Martin crouched broodingly next to her sturdy little Fiesta, but it was more to do with Quinn's hand at her elbow and the feel of his thigh next to hers than with the evening air.

Once in the luxurious confines of the car the faint but stomach-clenchingly seductive smell of Quinn's aftershave had her sitting stiff and straight in the leather seat, and it didn't help when Quinn leant over, brushing a wisp of hair from her forehead as he said quietly, 'Don't worry, you'll be fine. They are an easy bunch to get on with on the whole.'

He thought she was nervous about the evening ahead. The relief Candy experienced went some way to relaxing her tense muscles, and by the time the Aston Martin drew into the grounds of a very superior detached house she and Quinn were conversing easily. He had even made her laugh more than once as he related an amusing anecdote from a visit he'd made to one of the farms earlier in the day, when he had lost a battle with a particularly imposing and irate bullock who had taken exception to having a growth removed from its more intimate regions.

Harper had never really made her laugh. The thought came shooting out of the blue as Quinn stopped the car and left his seat to open her door for her, but as she watched the big, tall, dark figure walking round the bonnet of the Aston Martin she knew it was true. Harper had had great charisma—he'd been undeniably handsome and charming and everything a young girl could want—but he would no more have considered telling a story against himself like Quinn had just done than flying to the moon. Image had been everything with Harper; cool, macho man, always smooth and perfectly groomed.

She looked up at Quinn through her eyelashes as he opened the car door. Humour was important. She had heard Xavier make Essie laugh until she nearly cried, and she had noticed more than once that her uncle's wry and wicked wit was not unlike Quinn's.

She took the hand Quinn offered and slid gracefully out of the car, but as she straightened at the side of him he bent his dark head, whispering, 'You know that audience you spoke of...?' before he drew her into his arms and kissed her thoroughly. Very thoroughly. So thoroughly that her legs were like jelly and her heart was pounding under the black crêpe by the time he released her.

And then, before she could say anything, he had turned, drawing her in to the side of him as he said, his voice reflecting reserved politeness, 'Joanna, how are you? I don't think you have met Candy, have you? Candy Grey, Joanne Embleton-White.' There was a large, floridly handsome man just behind the tall, slim ash-blonde, and as Candy exchanged a flustered 'How do you do?' with the woman who had approached them, Quinn added, 'And this is Monty Hardingstone, the best accountant in the district. Monty, meet Candy.'

In contrast to Joanna Embleton-White, whose voice had held all the warmth of liquid ice, Monty's was hearty and his eyes approving as he said, 'So this is the little lady you've managed to snare, eh, Quinn? I can see why you didn't give the rest of us a chance. Nice to meet you, m'dear. Nice to meet you.'

'Thank you.' Candy managed to extricate her hand from Monty's vigorous grip after a moment or two and she carefully avoided looking at Joanna's face after one swift glance. The other woman's beautiful cold features had been stiff with annoyance.

The four of them walked across the drive and somehow Quinn managed to tuck her in to his side as though she was—what? Candy asked herself tautly. His girlfriend? His *mistress*? She tried to wriggle free once, but as his arm tightened round her waist like a band of steel she gave up the struggle, and listened to him making conversation with Monty with something like resignation.

However, there was nothing resigned about her face or voice when, on entering into the hall of the mansion, Candy found herself alone with Quinn for a second or two.

'Don't hold me like that,' she said quietly as her fingers prised at the arm round her waist.

'Like what?' was the calm rejoinder. 'You're supposed to be my loving girlfriend. Remember?'

'I know that, but—'

'No buts, Candy.' A pair of glittering ebony eyes in a dark, handsome face looked down at her, and as her breath caught in her throat Quinn said, 'If we're doing this we do it properly, okay? I'm a...physical man, and if you were my girlfriend I'd hold you like this and make sure that every other male in the vicinity knows you are mine. When I am with someone, I'm with someone. I don't believe in all this baloney about "open" relationships.'

'Neither do I,' she said indignantly. It had been as if he was accusing her of something.

'So, we both believe in faithfulness for as long as it lasts,' Quinn murmured softly. 'That's good, don't you think?'

'You're avoiding the issue and you know it,' she retorted huffily.

The dark eyes were laughing at her now, and he pulled her close for a moment, nuzzling her forehead with his chin as he said, 'Relax, Candy. It's a game, just a game; we both know that. But if we're playing it we play it for all it's worth. Agreed?'

'You're impossible. You know that, don't you?' She tried to frown at him but he was too handsome, too wicked, too *Quinn* for her to be really mad. And if she was being *really* honest, she admitted to herself silently, there was something very nice about being held and protected and loved by Quinn Ellington. Even if it was all just a show for the assembled crowd.

Candy enjoyed the rest of the evening although she hadn't expected to. There were a couple of less than comfortable moments, one of which being when Joanna cornered her in the downstairs cloakroom and managed to make a number of veiled hints as to her relationship with Quinn before Candy had arrived on the scene. Candy smiled sweetly, said little, and was gracious and charming, but it was something of an effort in the face of the other woman's covert hostility.

If nothing else it eliminated the faint sense of guilt she had felt at fooling Joanna and the rest, though. She knew Joanna's insinuations were without foundation—Quinn had been quite straightforward about his dislike of Joanna when she had questioned him about her after the episode on the drive, and very specific that he and the lovely blonde had never had so much as the whisper of an *amour*—but if she had really been his girlfriend, and the careful poison in Joanna's subtle remarks had done its job, she would have been feeling devastated.

As it was she lightly touched the other woman's arm on leaving the cloakroom, her voice mellow and her face sympathetic as she said, 'I'm sure Quinn will always look on you as a dear, dear friend, Joanna,' and left the blonde literally grinding her teeth in impotent fury.

When Meg Andrews entertained she did it in style, and there were twenty, including the hostess, seated at the magnificent table for dinner, which was a picture of gleaming silver cutlery, fine damask linen and sparkling crystal.

The conversation was witty and sharp, the endless courses delicious, and by the time she and Quinn left, just before midnight, several couples present had pressed invitations for the forthcoming Christmas celebrations upon them, all of which Quinn had seemed to accept, from what Candy could gather.

She broached the subject as soon as they were safely ensconced in the car.

'Quinn, how long had you envisaged this…tactic shall continue?' she asked carefully as he slid into the driving seat after settling her into the passenger seat as though she was breakable. Which was very pleasant. And seductive.

'Tactic?' He started the engine before turning to glance at her once, his ebony eyes narrowed.

'You know what I mean. This ploy about us being together,' she answered, just a little too sharply. 'It doesn't seem fair to keep it up.'

'No?' He expertly manoeuvred the car in a semicircle on the drive and let it purr gently towards the big gates in the distance. 'Unfair to whom, exactly?'

'Just…everyone. You said for an evening, remember?'

'Did I?' He sounded genuinely surprised, but Candy didn't trust him. She had seen a new side of Quinn tonight, and she was beginning to wonder if there were other facets of his complex personality just waiting to rear their heads.

'Yes, you did,' she said firmly.

'It's not a problem to continue a while longer, is it?' he asked in tones of patient reasonableness. 'You enjoyed yourself tonight, didn't you?'

'Of course I did, but that's not the point.'

'And it kept the lechers in check.'

'What?' Her head shot to look at his dark profile but Quinn was concentrating on easing the car on to the main road.

'You mean to say you didn't notice Monty drooling into his bow tie?' Quinn asked pleasantly. 'Or Brigadier Kealey panting at the leash?'

'I don't know what you're talking about.' She was honestly bewildered.

'Candy, those guys like you. Hell, any guy would like you. You're very...likeable.'

'Quinn—'

'It worked well tonight.' He did glance at her hot face then, one swift, all-encompassing glance. 'And nothing has changed as far as I can see. We both know what we want, and it doesn't include messy romantic involvements. I enjoyed being with you tonight and I had a great time. Can you say the same?'

'You know I can.'

'Then why spoil a good thing when there's no reason to? Neither of us have anyone on the horizon we're keen to date at the moment, but if that changed we both know where we stand. I'd like to think we could still be friends, though.' His voice was rational and quiet and there was no reason at all for Candy to want to do or say something outrageous to break that cool composure but she did. If all those other men—according to Quinn—found her so attractive, how come he was immune?

Was she being petty? She darted a swift glance at him from under her eyelashes. Probably, she admitted silently. And she wasn't normally like that. But then this wasn't exactly a normal situation, not as far as she was concerned at least. But as Quinn had pointed out neither of them were losing anything and they had everything to gain...didn't they? Oh, she wished she'd never started this ridiculous charade!

'Candy?' Quinn prompted lazily.

'Yes, fine, if you're happy to continue so am I,' she tossed back with detached coolness. 'I just didn't want to cramp your style, that's all.'

'There's no question of that. I've got a hell of a lot on my plate at the moment building the business up; the last thing I want is Joanna or someone similar causing problems.'

This was so cold-blooded. Candy suddenly felt totally drained, but she didn't intend to let Quinn see that. She casually fixed into place a loose curl that had come adrift from the carefully tousled knot on the top of her head, and then settled back in her seat before she said, 'In that case there's no problem.'

'Excellent.'

Quinn flashed her an approving smile and then turned back to the view beyond the windscreen. Why was he protracting this? He couldn't blame her for questioning it because he'd done the same thing himself. When he had first suggested this evening he'd had in mind a one-off—a way of introducing her into the social scene without there being any danger of someone frightening her off. She needed time to heal both physically and emotionally, that was what Essie had told him, and he could understand that. Apart from the physical trauma of the accident she had lost her fiancé; the man she had promised to spend the rest of her life with, the man she had loved and adored.

But she was too damn gorgeous for half the blokes round here to take that into consideration. His eyes narrowed on the road ahead as the surge of anger—he wouldn't allow himself to regard it as jealousy—that had burnt on and off all evening reared its head again at the memory of how it had been. The men had been sniffing round her all evening, damn 'em, and that was when she'd had the protection of being his girlfriend. What would it have been like if they'd known the truth? They had had all the finesse of rutting stags.

He found he was gripping the steering wheel with considerably more force than was necessary, and made a conscious decision to relax, taking several deep, silent breaths before he said, 'I should have checked with you before I accepted any other invitations though, Candy, especially in view of the fact that you might be spending Christmas at home?'

'Home?' Home was the cottage, with Tabitha and the kittens, and it was a second or two before it registered he meant Canada.

'Oh, no, I shan't be going home,' she said quickly. 'There's the cats to consider now.'

He could offer to board the cat and kittens at the practice for her but he didn't. What he did say was, 'In that case spend Christmas with me?'

He felt sorry for her, was that it? She thought about how he had remained at her side all evening rather than circulating, as most of the others had done, his arm round her waist for a good deal of the time and his manner if not possessive than certainly protective. Yes, he felt sorry for her. 'I don't think so,' she said pleasantly. 'I'm sure you're going to be very busy and I was looking forward to a quiet Christmas Day this year.'

'I don't think it will be a riot at my house,' he said with wry amusement.

'But you must have family to visit and so on?'

Should he tell her his parents were coming down to stay for a couple of days? His mother had been insistent that he have a decently cooked Christmas lunch when they'd discussed the holiday the last time he had popped up to Oxford in October, and it had been easier—certainly on his father, who bore the brunt of his mother's fretting and worrying—to invite them. But Candy would probably feel she was intruding if he said anything.

'I'm not visiting anyone,' Quinn said briskly, 'apart from the odd emergency patient, that is. They always crop up, Christmas or no Christmas, but Bob and Jamie are on the rota too, so it shouldn't be too disruptive. You can bring Tabitha and the kittens if you like. The dogs are perfectly accustomed to everything that crawls, walks, flutters or flies; they won't hurt them.'

'Thank you, but I don't think—'

'I would like you to come, Candy,' Quinn said very quietly.

Their eyes met for the briefest of moments as he turned his head to look at her, but it was enough to silence her protest and send hot colour surging into her cheeks.

He heard her draw a quick breath, and then her voice came as quietly as his when she said, 'All right, if you're sure.'

Sure? He was beginning to think he wasn't sure about anything, and he didn't like that. He didn't like it at all.

Candy had left a light on in the cottage, and the little glow from behind the curtains was welcoming as Quinn drew into the space beside the Fiesta.

'Would you like a coffee?' She had pondered all the way home on whether to ask.

'Some other time,' Quinn said evenly, 'but I'll just make sure everything's okay before I go.'

'Okay?' She had felt the refusal of coffee was a rebuff

in some way—she couldn't quite pin it down but there'd been something in his manner she hadn't liked—and now her voice was curt when she said, 'Why wouldn't it be okay? We've only been gone a few hours.'

'I don't know.' Quinn shrugged easily. 'Alfie wrecking the joint, something like that?'

'I don't need nursemaiding, Quinn.'

'I shall still see you to the door.' There was a touch of brusqueness in his voice and it startled her. 'I would do the same for any woman I was with so cut the touchiness.'

'Touchy? I'm not touchy,' Candy protested vehemently as Quinn opened his door.

He ignored her, walking round to the passenger side and opening her door without speaking, his face distant and cold.

'I am *not* touchy,' she repeated firmly when she was standing beside the car. 'It's just that I used to be on my own for huge amounts of time when I lived with Xavier and he was away on business. It doesn't worry me coming home to an empty house.'

'Good.' His voice was without expression and his face gave nothing away, and she stared at him for a moment, irritation vying with resentment. Why she let him get under her skin like this she didn't know, Candy thought crossly, her soft mouth tightening. And why she had promised to accompany him even one more time—let alone spend Christmas Day with him—she knew even less!

He took her arm as they walked towards the front door and she had to force herself not to jerk away, but his jibe had bitten deep and she was blowed if she was going to give him an excuse to repeat it.

Once she had opened the front door Quinn made a quick reconnoitre of the cottage and then returned to the threshold, where Candy was still standing, her hands on her hips and her face expressing resigned patience. 'Any mad axemen hiding under the bed or crazed psychopaths in the bathroom?' she asked sweetly.

He stared at her for one long moment and then he leant back against the open door, folding his arms across his chest and surveying her from under dark brows. 'You don't trust someone looking out for you, do you?' he stated softly. 'Why not?'

'What?' Her calm aplomb vanished in an instant.

'Or is it just me you don't trust?'

Tabitha, traitor that she was, was busily winding herself round Quinn's legs in an ecstasy of purring pleasure, and Candy bent quickly, lifting the sleek little cat into her arms to give herself time to think. But her thought process had frozen.

'I haven't the faintest idea what you are talking about,' she managed, after a moment of screaming silence.

'No?'

'No!'

'You are defensive and wary under that outward façade of woman of the world,' Quinn said with devastating directness. 'And I know you've been to hell and back with the accident and your fiancé dying, but it's more than that, isn't it?'

'Perhaps.' She stared into his eyes proudly as she found her tongue. 'But that's my business, Quinn, the same as the reason for your marriage breakdown is yours.'

Quinn shifted position slightly, his dark face showing no emotion whatsoever. 'Touché,' he said softly. 'Although I never said my marriage broke down, as I remember.'

'You said you had been married, and you don't have a wife with you now so what other assumption is there?' Candy asked coolly.

'My wife died, Candy, along with our baby son.'

'Oh, Quinn.' If the ground had opened and swallowed her it would have been a relief. She stared at him, her throat working and her mind searching for something, anything to say that would make amends. 'Quinn, I'm so *sorry*.'

He shrugged indifferently but the action didn't hide the pain stamped on his face. 'It wasn't a marriage made in heaven, as it happens,' he said with a tightness that was indicative of the emotion he was keeping under wraps. 'But that's another story.'

'Quinn, I shouldn't have said anything. I'm so sorry, I really am,' she stammered frantically, the colour that had flooded into her face leaving it just as quickly and showing her skin to be white with shock.

'It's all right.' And then, as she continued to stare at him with appalled eyes, Quinn reached out and took Tabitha from her, setting the cat on the floor before straightening and taking her arms in his hands as he faced her. 'It was three years ago,' he said quietly, 'and I'll tell you the story some time, but not now, not tonight. Okay?'

She nodded slowly, fighting back the tears. His son. His baby son. How did someone get over such a tragedy?

'And it was me that started the ball rolling so don't go putting on sackcloth and ashes,' he added huskily.

'Oh, Quinn.' She couldn't have described the tumult of emotion surging through every nerve and sinew but she had never felt so mixed up in all her life.

Quinn expelled a quiet breath, cupping her jaw gently with one hand. He had meant the kiss to be a brief farewell, a mere brushing of her lips before he left, but the second his mouth touched hers it changed to something different. Something warm and sensuous, heated, his fingers moving to tangle in her hair as he moved her close into his hard frame.

It took them both by surprise, the fire that shot between them, but it triggered sensations that fuelled more sensations, his tongue searching and exploring as her lips opened fully beneath his and her hands moved up round his neck.

Candy couldn't believe what she was experiencing as his hard body, the smell and feel of him, seemed to set her ablaze, and Quinn was holding her even tighter as his lips plundered hers. She was aware she was kissing him back with a kind of abandoned eagerness she wouldn't have thought possible, and his thighs were hard against hers, his hands stroking her back and causing soft little moans to rise and quiver in her throat as desire flooded through her blood like hot mulled wine.

As his tongue probed the secret places of her mouth she felt an electric current charge through her body, something alien and exciting and altogether overwhelming. She was alive in a way she had never been before and the knowledge was as frightening as it was thrilling. This power he had, she had never felt anything like this with Harper, not for a second. It was as though she had no will of her own, as though every curve and rounded part of her had been created to mould into the strong, tough angles and planes of his maleness.

She was trembling, she could feel it, and his heart was slamming against the wall of his chest like a sledgehammer.

It was Quinn who stopped and pulled away, his hands moving from stroking the small of her back and becoming restraining instead. She opened her eyes in bewilderment, still captivated by the new sensations he had aroused and half in the world of exploding colour and light he had created behind her closed lids. She stared at him, her eyes wide and dilated and her mouth bruised, and he returned the look, a mask sliding down over the naked passion.

'We're not thinking straight; it's the evening, the wine and the lateness of the hour,' he said thickly. 'I had better go.'

She looked at him blankly, utterly unable to respond with the light, defusing comment the situation called for.

'I'll give you a call about Jeff and Lynn's party next week, okay?' he continued after a moment or two.

'Okay.' It was a faint whisper but the best she could do.

And he nodded abruptly, his face rigid with control as he turned without another word, without even a goodbye, and strode down the path towards the car.

She shut the door before he had reached the gate, leaning against the wood for a moment with her eyes tightly shut and her heart pounding with the enormity of what had just happened. Fool, fool, fool! The words thudded in her head with ever increasing recrimination. She had behaved like a fool, worse than a fool.

All her fine words about the need for them to remain as just friends, to keep their distance, and she had practically *eaten* him.

'Oh, no...' She opened her eyes to stare into the room and met Tabitha's brilliant green gaze from where the cat had settled herself in the basket again with the sleeping kittens. You see what passion does? it seemed to say as the cat lowered her head to her family. Here today and gone tomorrow.

Candy levered herself off the door and walked into the kitchen, plugging in the kettle and making herself a strong cup of instant coffee with hands that were shaking. She felt cheap. Cheap and ridiculous. And she had never felt like that before in all her life, not even in the fiasco of the few minutes before the crash when Harper had admitted he had been using her all along.

Quinn had been totally up front with her from day one. He had made it crystal-clear that the last thing on his agenda—the very last—was any thought of commitment or a permanent relationship with anyone, and what had she done? Virtually invited him into her bed! And it had been Quinn who had stopped. Quinn who had walked away. Oh, hell...

She drank the coffee straight down and made herself another cup, drinking it curled on the thick rug by the cat basket as she stroked the purring Tabitha and watched the drowsy kittens' enchanting little faces.

She felt better after a while. They had just kissed, she told herself firmly. All right, so it had been passionate, mind-blowing, but nevertheless it *had* been just a kiss. They had been entwined so closely she had felt every inch of him against her as though they were naked, but they *hadn't* been naked. The taste, the feel, the smell of him was stamped on her so indelibly she felt she would never be the same again, but a bath, a good night's sleep, and she *would* awake feeling like Candy Grey again.

She had to keep a sense of proportion about this.

It was another ten minutes before she went upstairs and ran herself a hot bath, generously laced with a madly expensive bubble bath she normally kept for special occasions, in Essie's pretty little bathroom. She undressed quickly, flinging the black dress and underwear in a corner of the bedroom and padding through to the bathroom stark naked, there to lie in the warm, silky water for nearly thirty minutes.

It took her over an hour to drift into an exhausted sleep once she was in bed and even then she didn't sink deeply into slumber immediately, but skimmed in and out of vivid, disturbing dreams where she was chasing someone, endlessly, through confusing dark corridors, until the beginnings of a pink-edged dawn began to make itself known.

She awoke then, padded into the bathroom and drank a glass of water and returned to bed, and this time dropped into a deep, dreamless sleep where there were no yesterdays, no tomorrows, just welcome oblivion.

CHAPTER FIVE

IT TOOK every ounce of Candy's will-power to sound cool and calm and collected when Quinn phoned the cottage the next day. She had finally surfaced just after eleven, and after a perfunctory toilet had dressed quickly in jeans and a thick jumper, bundled her hair into a ponytail and left to fetch the Sunday papers.

Once home again, and with the fire blazing, she had settled down on the sofa with the papers and a cup of coffee, before fixing herself a light lunch of cheese omelette and cold meat, which she ate in front of the fire with Tabitha on the sofa at the side of her helping her out with the home-cured ham and chicken.

She had bought a furry clockwork mouse the week before for Alfie and his sisters, Jemima and Poppy, along with a couple of other small toys, and the entertainment the trio provided through the winter afternoon was better than any TV.

Teatime came and went, and Candy resolutely avoided glancing at the telephone, but then when it rang, at eight o'clock in the evening, her stomach jumped into her mouth and she knew she had been waiting for this moment all day. Of course it might not be Quinn, she told herself as she lifted the receiver. He had said he would call her but he hadn't been specific as to when.

'Candy?' The deep, dark voice was smooth and friendly. 'Hi, it's Quinn.'

'Hallo, Quinn.' Hallo, Quinn. She felt an almost hysterical urge to giggle at the calmness of her voice when she had been turning herself inside out half the night over this man. She gripped the receiver tightly and said coolly, 'Thanks again for a lovely evening last night. It was great to meet everyone.'

'My pleasure.'

Oh, they were being *so* polite, but that was better than performing a painful and embarrassing post-mortem that would help neither of them, Candy thought soberly.

'There's a few of us meeting for a drink in the Saddler's Arms in half an hour,' Quinn said easily, 'and I wondered if you were free to join us. I could pick you up if you like?'

She moved the telephone away from her ear and stared blankly at it for a second or two. Last night hadn't affected him one tiny bit! Here she'd been, in a state of controlled dithering all day, unable to paint or to put her mind to anything, and he was as cool as a cucumber. She didn't know whether she wanted to laugh or cry, but in the event she called on her considerable source of pride and said pleasantly, 'That would have been nice but I'm in the middle of something. Can I take a raincheck?'

'Sure. Look, I'm on call for the rest of the week, so I doubt if I'll get the chance to phone again. About Jeff and Lynn's party on Saturday? I'll pick you up round eightish, if that's okay?'

She took a long, deep breath and then said brightly, 'Absolutely, I'll be ready. Goodbye, Quinn.'

The briefest of pauses, and then, 'Goodbye, Candy.'

Candy sat looking at the telephone for a full minute after she had replaced the receiver. He was an unfeeling brute. All right, so he'd looked devastated when he'd spoke about his wife and son, but as far as now was concerned, as far as *she* was concerned, he couldn't care less. It wasn't an exaggeration to say that his lovemaking last night had been the most shattering experience of her whole life and it had left him cold. Emotionally at least. He'd certainly been physically turned on, she thought with a measure of bitter satisfaction, although even then it had been Quinn who had called a halt.

She shook her head, sucking in then expelling an irritable sigh. Enough of this! She wasn't going to waste one more minute worrying about Quinn Ellington. He had set the ground rules and she would make sure they kept to them from now on. Never, *never* would she put herself in such a vulnerable position again. Last night had been a definite one-off and if he thought differently then she would put him wise in no uncertain terms. Escort—fine, friend—fine, lover—no way.

Over the next three weeks until Christmas it became clear that Quinn had no intention of repeating his brief lapse from being strictly platonic.

They went to Jeff and Lynn's party and Candy found she enjoyed herself thoroughly, and when Quinn took her home his inspection of the cottage was brief and cool and he had gone before she knew it, with nothing more controversial than a brief peck on her cheek.

She joined Quinn and some of his friends at the Saddler's Arms the following evening, when he repeated his invitation from the week before, but she insisted on driving herself and meeting Quinn there.

Quinn was the epitome of the attentive boyfriend whilst they had an audience, but when he walked her out to her car parked at the rear of the little old-fashioned pub, which was all brass and leaded windows and oak beams, he merely brushed her forehead with his lips—as though she was five years old, Candy thought resentfully—and waved her goodbye.

And so it continued, through an evening out with Jeff and Lynn to the cinema and a meal afterwards, another party—at Colonel Llewellyn's beautiful home this time—and finally a Christmas dinner the night before Christmas

Eve at Marion's home, with Jamie and his girlfriend making up a sixsome with Marion and her portly little husband.

On each occasion Candy enjoyed herself immensely and then, once she was home again and alone with Tabitha and the kittens, found herself pacing the cottage in a state of restless agitation for half the night. And she didn't understand why. Unless it was the strain of keeping up the pretence? she questioned on the morning of Christmas Eve, when she awoke late and found herself reluctant to leave the enveloping warmth of her bed.

And it was a strain, she admitted with a tired sigh as she snuggled back under the covers for another five minutes of wicked luxury. She had never been any good at acting a part since she had been cast as Mary in the school nativity play when she was five years old, and had frozen at her first sight of the sea of smiling faces and left poor Joseph to make his way to Bethlehem alone. But it wasn't just her fear of inadvertently saying something that would give the game away. She shut her eyes tightly. It was him. Quinn.

If he had been just a little less handsome, a little less good company, if he had had no sense of humour or been a typical macho man, picked his nose, *anything*, she could have coped.

As it was...she found herself as jumpy as a cat on a hot tin roof half the time, and it was exhausting. Her whole insides tensed every time he touched her and as his pretend girlfriend he touched her a lot. And each time it happened she remembered what it had felt like to be in his arms, tasting him, feeling him, smelling him...

She sat up abruptly, brushing back her mass of silky red hair with an impatient hand. Last night, when he had sat beside her on one of Marion's cosy two-seater sofas after dinner, his hard thigh pressed close to hers and his arm stretched out casually at the back of her, which brought him even closer, she had decided that once Christmas was over she would tell him the deal was off.

She hugged her knees, her azure-blue gaze narrowed across the room. There might be women out there who could treat Quinn Ellington in a buddy-buddy fashion— although she doubted it—but she wasn't one of them. Whenever she was with him she felt such a see-saw of emotions she didn't recognise herself. Awkward, elated, unwanted, cherished, gauche or shamefully wanton! The list was endless and each one contradictory. She had never felt any of this with Harper.

She had been happy with Harper, happy and comfortable. There had been none of these exhausting swings of emotion that left her confused and miserable each time Quinn left. Harper hadn't disturbed something deep inside like Quinn did.

She paused abruptly in her thinking, her stomach churning faintly as though her mind was trying to tell her something her heart didn't want to hear. Her brow wrinkled and she dismissed the unease firmly. The difference was because Harper had been her finacé and Quinn was— Well, she didn't know what he was exactly, she admitted ruefully. Boyfriend? Definitely not, by his own volition. Companion? Certainly the most disconcerting one she had ever had. Friend? No, she couldn't look on Quinn as a friend, whatever he said. Friends didn't disturb your sleep pattern and send you half crazy.

'Enough, Candy Grey.' She spoke out loud into the room and then wagged her head lugubriously at herself. He'd got her talking to herself now, first sign of madness! Yes, she would definitely call off this ridiculous farce once Christmas was over. She had known Quinn for two months, and in that time she had come to realise he was a highly discriminating and intelligent individual on top of everything else. He would understand the game had gone on long enough, but just in case he was put out at all she wouldn't rock the boat before the holiday was over. She owed him a pleasant and relaxed Christmas.

Candy worked for the rest of the day. She had finished the painting Quinn had admired some two weeks before and had decided to do a series of snow scenes which could either be sold as a collection or individually. It was warm and snug in the cottage, with the fire sending red and gold flames flickering cosily up the chimney and the cats playing at her feet, but there had been the smell of snow in the air when she had fetched more logs and coal from the potting shed earlier. The sky was low and heavy with it, she thought about four in the afternoon, when she peered out of the cottage window as the light began to fail rapidly. It looked as if all the forecasts of a white Christmas were going to come true.

It was just as the first fat white flakes began to fall from the laden sky some twenty minutes later that she heard Quinn's Discovery in the lane outside the cottage, and she raised her head from cleaning her paints in surprise. As far as she knew Quinn had been going to pick her and the cats up at ten in the morning. Whatever was he doing here now? Had he come to tell her the arrangement was off for some reason?

She refused to accept the bitter pang of disappointment which accompanied the thought and instead walked to the door, opening it just as Quinn reached the doorstep.

'Hi.' Quinn's flagrant masculinity was very pronounced today, with the black denim jeans and bulky waist-length black leather jacket he was wearing, and the word came out breathlessly, although she did better with, 'Don't tell me. The local animal population has decided they need you more than me tomorrow?' as she forced a bright smile.

He smiled in return—a warm and fascinatingly sexy

smile, Candy thought a touch resentfully—as he said, 'Not at all. May I come in?'

'Oh, yes, of course, come in. I was just going to make a coffee,' she added quickly, 'would you like one?'

'Would a drowning man refuse a helping hand?'

'Here, help yourself.' She passed him the tin of chocolate chip cookies across the breakfast bar as Quinn seated himself on one of the high stools on the sitting room side of the bar, and after switching on the kettle and spooning coffee into two china mugs she turned to face him again. 'Hard day?' she asked carefully.

'Long day.' He grimaced. 'I was called out to Breedon's farm at two in the morning and haven't been to bed since. Old man Breedon has this big four-year-old chestnut. Beautiful beast of a horse, but like many highly-strung animals he has his likes and dislikes, and one of the latter is needles.'

'And you had to…?'

'Inject him, yes. He'd managed to rip his shoulder on a loose piece of wood in his stable. Breedon had been out on some sort of shindig with the local golf fraternity and looked in on the horse before he went to bed. He'd had a skinful—Breedon, not the chestnut,' he added, with a grin that made her knees go weak, 'and in his intoxicated state decided he couldn't wait until a more civilised hour to call out the vet. Anyway, once I'd done the job he was so grateful he decided I had to sample a taste of some old malt whisky he'd got, and then we sat before the fire talking for hours, and his wife is always up early and does a full cooked breakfast…'

'A few hours' sleep would have done you more good.'

'I hate getting into a cold bed at some unearthly hour in the morning when I've been out,' he said matter-of-factly as he bit into another cookie after shrugging off the leather jacket.

Of course. He'd probably be remembering what it had been like when his wife was alive to welcome him back into her arms. The shaft of pain was as sharp as it was unexpected, and it caused her voice to be abrupt as she said, 'Is this a social call, or was there something specific you wanted to see me about?'

'Both.'

Clear as mud! But then every moment with Quinn was like this, so perhaps she shouldn't expect anything different? Candy asked herself silently. She waited until he had finished the biscuit and then said, 'Well?' before he reached for another.

'You've heard the forecast?' He nodded towards the window as he spoke, through which they could see the snow coming down in a thick white mantle now.

'Yes?'

'They say we're in for a packet, so I was thinking...' He paused, taking a long gulp of the coffee she had just handed him, 'I was thinking it would be easier all round if you came tonight and planned to stay for a couple of days. This lane isn't great at the best of times, but after a heavy fall of snow it's plain murder.'

'Stayed?' She stared at him blankly. 'With you, do you mean?'

'No, with the village postman,' he returned drily. 'Of course with me. Who else?'

She could think of at least a hundred people she would prefer to stay with rather than Quinn, and what would people think? She spoke the last out loud as she said, 'I couldn't possibly, Quinn. People would assume...'

'Yes?' He surveyed her over the rim of his mug, his black eyes glittering. 'What would people assume?'

'That we were, well, sleeping together,' she said uneasily.

'Would that be so terrible?' he murmured cryptically. 'We are supposed to be in a relationship, don't forget.'

Right, she had had just about enough of this, Candy thought militantly. The cheek of the man was colossal. 'But we aren't, are we?' she bit back tightly. 'And in spite of this modern age in which we live I don't particularly want my reputation to be—' She stopped abruptly.

'What?' he asked with genuine bewilderment.

'Sullied.'

'Sullied?' He was eyeing her now as though she was mad. 'What on earth are you talking about, Candy? People don't care a jot about that sort of thing these days.'

'I do.' She had gone very white but she was looking straight into his irritable face. 'I do, Quinn.'

'I don't believe I am hearing this,' he rasped exasperatedly. 'You'll be telling me next you don't believe in sex before marriage!' And then, at the look on her face, 'Good grief, you don't, do you?'

To hide her acute embarrassment and the surge of pain sweeping through her Candy glared at him, her eyes stormy and dark as she spat, 'What I believe and don't believe is nothing at all to do with you.'

'I disagree.'

'Tough!'

'Now look here, Candy—'

And then she knew she was going to lose it, big time. It was the superior look on his handsome face, the almost condescending stance he was taking. It was too much for Candy's over-sensitised nerves.

'You have no idea—no idea at all, do you?' she bit out with savage fury. 'I had to live with the results of what an immoral lifestyle can do to someone.'

'Immoral?' He stiffened, his face darkening. 'I'm not talking about immorality for crying out loud.'

'That all depends on how you look at it,' she hissed

furiously. 'My grandmother slept with a whole string of boyfriends before she married my grandfather, and then they had only been together for a short while before she ran off to Canada with his best friend when she realised she had fallen pregnant with the other man's child—my mother. He stayed around for a few months but he was soon gone, and then it was open house. Any man, any time! When Xavier was born my grandmother didn't have a clue who the father was and I don't think she even cared either. It was my mother who brought him up, and then when she was fourteen some drunken pig my grandmother had brought back to the house raped her. She died nine months later, bringing me into the world.'

'Candy, stop this.' Quinn was appalled; not by what she was revealing but by the look of raw pain on her face.

'Our name was notorious in the town where we lived.' Candy knew she ought to stop, but no power on earth could have prevented her from spilling it all. 'I was always known as the granddaughter of the Grey woman, even after Xavier had made his first million and moved us to the sort of place he had only dreamt of as a child living in dirt and squalor. Give a dog a bad name and it's kinder to hang him. That's what I learnt.'

'Not all people are like that, Candy.'

'I made up my mind as a teenager, when the first boyfriend to take me out groped me in the back of his car thinking I was like my grandmother, that I would never let any man treat me like that again,' Candy raged. 'He got nasty when I said no, and he said bad things, awful things, about my mother too. No one believed she had been raped, or if they did it was the general opinion she must have asked for it, being my grandmother's daughter.'

'But your fiancé wasn't like that, surely?' Quinn asked quietly. He wanted to go and comfort her, to take her in his arms and soothe the desperate pain and anguish, but he knew it would be the wrong time for any physical contact. And he was experiencing his own emotional upheaval too. It bothered him more than he would have thought possible that she had been hurt like this.

'Harper?' It was so bitter it made him flinch. 'Oh, Harper was a sweetheart all right. He never put a foot wrong—or a hand,' she added with acidic sarcasm. 'He respected me; he wanted to cherish and look after me; he wanted me for his wife. What he really wanted was a free meal ticket for the rest of his life! He knew Xavier thought the world of me and it was common knowledge, before Xavier met Essie, that he was against marriage. Harper thought I would get it all one day.

'But he didn't see why he should miss out until our wedding night and so he played around, often, but he got caught with one of his affairs—the woman got pregnant. That was the news he gave me the night of the crash, and it was through shouting at me, because I wouldn't go back on my decision that we were finished, that he didn't notice the lorry that had jackknifed across the road until it was too late. He swerved, went off the road, and the rest—as they say—is history.'

Quinn swore, softly but with such intensity that it jerked Candy out of the near hysteria into trembling silence.

'I'm sorry, Candy.' His voice was deep and sincere and carried a pain all of its own. 'I'm sorry you met such a low-down rat when you were too young to recognise him for what he was, and I'm sorry he broke your heart. But don't let him break your inner strength.'

'I won't.' Her lower lip was wobbling but she was determined she wasn't going to cry as she looked back at him. She couldn't believe she had told him the one thing she had sworn never to tell a living soul, and she would have given anything to take it back now the storm of rage and bitterness had blown itself out. He had told her he didn't want to get involved with her, he had made it so plain she would never have any part in his life beyond that of temporary 'friend', and here she had blurted out her worst humiliation and pain.

'Look, I should have told you straight off. My parents are at my house.' Quinn had called Harper a rat but he was acknowledging if there were any prizes going in that area he'd be first in line. Why hadn't he told her straight away that they wouldn't be alone? he asked himself, already knowing the answer but disliking the bitter taste it left on his tongue. Because she had annoyed him with her obvious distaste at the possibility people might assume their relationship was a serious one, serious enough for her to stay with him for a few days anyway. Pride, stinking male pride, he told himself silently, and the result was he had damn near broken her. But he just hadn't known she was so damaged.

'Your parents?' She was openly astonished and he couldn't blame her. 'You mean they are staying with you?'

'Just for a couple of days.' He had never felt such a heel. 'So if you want to come no one would think anything.'

'But...' She didn't understand any of this. 'Did you know they were coming?' she asked shakily. What was he thinking? What could she say? She had just made the biggest fool of herself ever, revealed all there was to know about herself, including—here she wanted to shut her eyes and sink through the floor—that she was a virgin, and all the time his *parents* had been sitting back at the practice?

'Yes, I knew they were coming.'

'Why didn't you tell me?' she asked weakly. 'Was it a last-minute thing?'

'No, they've been coming for weeks, but I thought if I told you you would make some excuse not to come, and—and I didn't want you spending Christmas alone.'

Xavier and Essie. The rage that swept through her now

was white-hot, and made the anger of a few minutes before seem mild in comparison. They had put pressure on him, no doubt, with this nursemaiding notion that he had to keep an eye on her. It was this very thing that had caused all the trouble in the first place!

She drew herself up now, moving away from the cupboard against which she had been leaning and walking through into the sitting room before turning to face him. 'Quinn, I wouldn't spend Christmas with you if you were the last man on earth,' she said bitterly. Pity he could keep; she didn't want it!

'Wrong.' His eyes had narrowed as he in his turn had moved to stand in front of her, but otherwise his expression had remained exactly the same. 'You are coming.'

'Over my dead body.'

'Don't be childish.' The slanting of her vivid blue eyes told him that was the wrong tack to take, but he wasn't prepared for her hand to come shooting out and hit him hard across the face.

'Get out.' She had gone very white. '*Now.*' And then she horrified them both by bursting into tears.

Quite how she found herself sitting on his lap in the chair as she wailed against the charcoal silk of his shirt Candy didn't know, and at first it didn't matter. She was too devastated, too shaken by the enormity of the whole scene which had erupted, and especially her actually having had the temerity to strike Quinn, to care, but then, after a few minutes of wild sobbing, she became disturbingly aware of hard muscled flesh beneath the silk, and the soothing, guttural sounds coming from his throat.

He was wearing the clean, sharp aftershave she had smelt before, and it was undeniably sexy. *He* was undeniably sexy. And the chain reaction his closeness was setting off in her body had nothing to do with comfort and friendship and all to do with something much more base and carnal.

She swallowed hard, forcing the hiccuping sobs to quieten as she raised her head from his shoulder. 'I've made your shirt wet.' She kept her eyes on the damp patch just under his shoulder on his chest as she spoke; she didn't dare to look at him.

'It will dry.' His voice was husky, but as she rose unsteadily to her feet he made no attempt to stop her. Quinn Ellington was coping with feelings new to him, savage, threatening feelings, and they were as emotional as they were physical. He wanted this woman. Physically he wanted her more than he had ever wanted any other woman in his life, and that included Laura. Laura had fallen into his hands like a ripe peach, and at the time he had been arrogant enough to expect it; from puberty he had found the female sex only too willing to jump into his bed.

He had never waited for a woman before, but now he knew that was what he had been doing from day one with Candy. He had pushed the knowledge down deep somewhere, burying it under the guise of getting to know her, but really he had been biding his time. He wanted her in his bed, that was the truth of it, but she was Essie's hurt fledgling, and as such he had told himself she needed time to recover. And then...well, she would be just like all the others, of course. *Fool.*

He watched her as she walked across the room with a muttered remark about washing her face, and then she had gone upstairs and he was alone.

After all she had revealed he couldn't take her into his bed knowing that in a few months they would be going their separate ways. She was too vulnerable, too insecure after her miserable childhood and painful adolescence to do that.

He rose from the chair; the closeness of her, the scent of her skin and the soft silk of her hair had made him rockhard and he needed to cool down.

Tabitha wound round his legs as he walked to the door and he bent, briefly stroking the cat and Alfie, who had darted quickly after his mother, before opening the door and stepping outside into the white, feather-soft snow-filled night. The snow was falling thickly now, already the ground was a pale, sparkling carpet, and he stood outside drawing in cleansing lungfuls of the bitingly cold air before walking over to the Discovery and hauling the cat carriers he had brought from the surgery out of the back of the big vehicle.

As he walked back into the cottage the telephone began to ring, and, seeing that Candy was still upstairs, he put the carriers by the door and walked across to lift the receiver, stating the number as he did so.

There was a moment's pause the other end, and then a female voice said uncertainly, 'Quinn? Is that you?'

'Essie?'

'Oh, it is you!' Quinn could tell she was smiling by the sound of her voice. 'I'm so glad Candy isn't by herself on Christmas Eve. Is she there?'

'Powdering her nose,' Quinn said shortly. 'Look, I invited her to come and spend a couple of days with me over Christmas—the weather is expected to be bad, deep snow, and as my parents are in residence I thought we might make a little party of it. She's not too keen, so put in your two pennyworth, would you?' Okay, so it was sneaky, but he needed all the help he could get.

'Oh, yes, all right.' There was a slightly longer pause this time, before Xavier's wife said, 'Quinn? There's nothing wrong, is there?'

There wasn't anything that was right! 'No, everything's great,' he lied cheerfully. 'I think I can hear Candy coming; I'll just tell her it's you.'

Candy was halfway down the stairs when he called to her, and her face had a scrubbed, soap and water look to it. He remembered how her body had felt as she had nestled on his lap, and all the good work the cold outside had done was lost. 'It's Essie,' he said evenly, jerking his head at the phone. 'I've told her you are coming to me for Christmas and she is thrilled you aren't going to be here by yourself, so don't worry her by saying anything different.'

'Quinn—'

'Remember the baby,' he warned softly.

'That's emotional blackmail,' she sniffed weakly, the hot retort she had been about to make dying on her lips as she noticed the vivid mark of her hand across one bronzed cheekbone. She had never hit anyone before and she had had to start with Quinn! And it had been no light tap either.

By the end of the conversation with Essie she acknowledged it was a *fait accompli*. Essie had enthused it would make her Christmas—as it would Xavier's—that Candy was with friends over the holiday. They had been just the tiniest bit worried about her, Essie had confided gently, but, knowing she was with Quinn, she and Xavier could relax. They had been pleased when she had told them she was having Christmas lunch with Quinn some weeks back, but this made so much more sense if the weather forecast was bad.

Candy spoke to Xavier next, and just hearing her uncle's voice made the lump in her throat grapefruit size. They chattered for a few minutes and then Xavier asked to speak to Quinn.

The men's conversation was brief and succinct and consisted mainly of monosyllables on Quinn's part.

'What did he say?' Candy asked hesitantly when Quinn put the phone down. She had told herself during the call she wasn't going to ask but she couldn't help it.

'He merely expressed fatherly concern as to my intentions,' Quinn said shortly, one dark eyebrow raised in a quizzical fashion as he glanced her way.

'He's not my father.' It was pithy, but she was sick of everyone poking their noses in her business, Candy told herself aggressively. She wasn't a child!

And that was exactly what Quinn made her feel—a spoilt, irrational child—when he said calmly, 'He loves you, Candy, and so does Essie. You can't blame them for being interested in your welfare.'

She could! Oh, yes, she could. This present sorry situation had come about by Xavier and Essie's interest in her welfare! She was a grown woman of twenty-four and she had been used to looking after herself for a long time—she hadn't *needed* them to ask Quinn to be her guardian angel! Her face reflected the fruit of her thoughts, and as he caught her scowl Quinn eyed her reprovingly. 'You'll have lines before you're thirty,' he said with irritating equability.

'Well, you won't have to look at them so it doesn't matter much one way or the other,' Candy said tartly, catching sight of the cat carriers as she spoke, which caused her face to darken further. He was so sure of himself!

Quinn's mouth twisted as he followed her glance and she knew he had read her mind accurately.

'Throw a few things into a case and get your brood ready and we'll be off.' He glanced at her as he spoke, noticing the defiant tilt to her head as she stared back at him.

'I told you. I'm not coming.'

'And what about your promise to Essie?'

'I never promised her a thing,' Candy said sharply. 'You had told them I was coming to stay with you and I didn't contradict it, that's all. They are far enough away to remain in blissful ignorance unless you tell them different, which I'm sure you won't do...in view of the baby,' she added sarcastically.

'And my parents?' Quinn asked flatly. 'You're quite happy to ruin their Christmas? They are expecting me to bring my girlfriend to meet them, so when I go back and say we're no longer an item how do you think that is going to make them feel?'

'You should have thought of that before you said I'd stay.'

But her voice was no longer so certain, and Quinn was quick to ruthlessly press the advantage her soft heart had given him. 'Candy, my mother all but had a nervous breakdown when Laura and her grandson were killed three years ago,' he said quietly, his voice having the advantage of the ring of truth. 'Since then...well, I've dated occasionally over the last year or so but there has never been anyone special. She was so pleased when I mentioned your name.'

'You—!' She swore, a very modest swear-word, but it was so unlike her she blushed scarlet as she continued, 'That's terrible, Quinn. How could you do that to her when you know this is just a façade we're putting up?'

'I didn't realise it would affect her the way it has,' Quinn said soberly. 'At the time of the accident they hid most of their distress for my sake; it was only when I mentioned you that my father told me later how thrilled she was and what it meant to her that I was recovering—' He stopped abruptly.

'It was bad for a time?' Candy asked softly, before mentally kicking herself at the banality of the words. His wife and his son had violently been snatched from him and she asked him if it was bad!

But Quinn didn't seem to find the question trite. 'Yes, it was bad,' he said heavily. 'The worst.'

'I'm sorry, Quinn.' And she was, desperately so. 'Of course I'll come and stay. But—'

'What?' The black eyes were unblinking as they honed in on her troubled blue gaze.

'After Christmas, when they've gone home, we need to have a talk,' she said flatly. 'Agreed?'

'Agreed.' He smiled, a sexy quirk of his mouth that was

quite natural and therefore ten times more attractive, and he walked over to her, reaching out and splaying his hands round her waist as he pulled her against him for a moment, dropping a light kiss on her nose. 'After Christmas,' he said silkily.

'I mean it, Quinn.' She could feel his fingertips against her lower ribs through the long-sleeved jersey top she was wearing, and the strength and warmth of his gentle forcefulness was seductive, much, much too seductive for her fragile equilibrium.

'Absolutely,' he agreed with suspect meekness.

She drew in a deep breath, wondering how on earth she had been so criminally insane as to think this idea could ever have worked in the first place. A platonic friendship with Quinn? You might as well ask a girl to stop breathing.

'Good.' She pushed away from him but he wasn't quite ready to let her go.

'Harper must have been crazy,' he said softly, looking down into the brilliant blue of her eyes.

'Yes, well, he obviously didn't think so,' she returned weakly, trying again to ease herself out of his grip but with no success.

'Do Essie and Xavier know about his other women?' He was remembering the note in Xavier's voice earlier and thinking that it was probably just as well Harper wasn't around any longer or else Xavier might be facing a prison sentence!

'No, no one does except you.'

There was a split second's silence and then Quinn said, 'I'm glad you trusted me enough to tell me, Candy.'

'I didn't intend to,' she said tightly, 'and I'm not at all sure I trust you, if you really want to know.'

There was another silence, and then Quinn began to laugh, really laugh, his head thrown back as he fairly roared.

'You certainly have a way of bringing the male ego down a peg or two, don't you?' he said amusedly when he had control again.

'I think your ego is quite able to look after itself.' Candy's voice was severe and she hadn't laughed. 'Would you let go of me now, please?'

'Why? I think this is rather nice,' he said comfortably.

So did she, and that was exactly why she had made the request! 'Nice isn't always good,' she said firmly.

'True.' His head was tilted now and the ebony eyes were laughing at her again. 'But in this case...'

He didn't prolong the kiss, and it wasn't at all like the other time, but nevertheless Candy's knees were melting by the time he let her go with a casual, 'Go and pack your case, then, and I'll sort out the moggies.'

She wanted to remind him that they were just friends, that whatever he had told his parents it didn't alter the basic rules of their arrangement, but somehow, in the face of his utter nonchalance, she couldn't find any words that wouldn't make her seem prim and gauche and strait-laced in objecting to the kiss. And so she bit her lip, lifted her chin and marched off to pack her case with as much dignity as she could muster.

CHAPTER SIX

CANDY liked Quinn's parents straight away. Mary Ellington was a surprisingly tiny, pretty woman, her thick mass of snow-white hair in stark contrast to her face, which was still relatively unlined, and her husband was an older version of Quinn.

Their greeting was warm, too warm for Candy's feelings of guilt, and when Mary said, her voice hesitant, 'I started getting the tea ready, I do hope you don't mind?' the guilt intensified tenfold.

'Of course not.' Candy managed a fairly normal smile. The other woman was obviously nervous of treading on Quinn's 'girlfriend's' toes. Little did she know it was the first time she had been invited to Quinn's flat above the practice, Candy thought helplessly.

And what a flat it was! Her first impression, as she had stepped into the enormous sitting room, had been one of aggressive luxury and beautiful co-ordination. The deep pile silver-grey carpet, the magnificent charcoal leather suite and no-nonsense furnishings were relentlessly masculine. There were no soft touches, no hint of a woman's taste anywhere. Even the Christmas cards had been slotted into a little cardboard tree that was more practical than festive, and other than that slight concession it wouldn't have been apparent what the season was.

Candy thought of the cottage, and the cards she had strung up round the walls downstairs, and the little pine tree complete with baubles that the cats had been having the time of their lives wrecking as soon as her back was turned, and felt sad. This place screamed aloneness.

And then she reminded herself, very quickly, that Quinn had mentioned on the drive to the practice that the flat was very much as Xavier had left it.

He had been far too busy, Quinn had explained, to bother changing things, besides which he liked Xavier's taste and would probably have chosen the same colour scheme and furnishings himself anyway.

The dogs were apparently all kept downstairs in the back of the house at night, and so when Quinn brought the two cat carriers in there was plenty of oohing and ahhing from his parents when they saw the kittens, which all four cats revelled in. Quinn had even thought to provide a litter tray and feeding bowls in a recess off the kitchen, and before long the four cats had made themselves perfectly at home and were curled up in the wicker basket, which Quinn had also thought to bring, in front of the gas fire.

When Candy followed Mary into the kitchen to help get the meal ready a few minutes later she found it was a chef's paradise, but with a curiously unlived-in air. Everything was immaculate—and Quinn's mother had clearly been thinking along the same lines because her first words, once they were alone, were, 'Quinn doesn't eat properly, does he? And it does *so* worry me. Bernard tells me to stop fussing but I can't help it. That's what mothers do, isn't it?'

Mary smiled a smile that begged for understanding of her maternal anxiety, and there was something in the other woman's sweet face that made Candy forgo the polite remark she had been about to make and say instead, 'I don't really know what mothers do, mine died when I was born, but if I was a mother I think I would be feeling the same as you do.'

'Oh, my dear, I'm so sorry.' Mary laid a small comforting hand on Candy's arm. 'How dreadful for you. Quinn never said.'

The trouble was she didn't have a clue what Quinn *had* told his parents—or what he hadn't told them, which was perhaps even more relevant, Candy warned herself silently.

And as the evening progressed it became apparent that Quinn's mother was very definitely sold on the idea that her son had made a love-match. Mary was discreet—the older woman didn't have an injudicious bone in her body, Candy thought fondly—but there was just the odd little remark, a glance, a certain gleam in her eyes that indicated what Quinn's mother was thinking.

And it made Candy feel conscience-stricken, ashamed, remorseful to fool such nice people, which was so *unfair* she told herself bitterly, when this whole giant tangle could be laid fairly and squarely at Quinn's size tens.

Mary had insisted on bringing enough food with her to feed an army for a week, and once they had eaten the evening meal—a truly delicious ham and egg pie of Mary's, with baked potatoes smothered with a blue cheese dip—the two women left the men in the sitting room watching TV and drinking port, and went into the kitchen to prepare the vegetables and stuffing they were having with the enormous turkey Quinn's parents had also provided.

They were laughing at the story Candy was telling about Quinn under the hawthorn bush when the man himself walked into the kitchen some time later, and as both women turned to him, their faces alight and their eyes bright with shared amusement, the words he had been about to say died on his lips and he stood in the doorway looking as though he was stunned.

'Quinn?' Candy stared at him, the laughter fading from her face. 'What's the matter? Don't you feel well?'

'What?' And then he seemed to collect himself, the smooth, relaxed mask he was apt to wear sliding into place as he said, 'No, I'm fine. I just came to say I've brought your case up and put it in your room, that's all.'

'Thank you.' She continued staring at him, puzzled.

'Well, once we've finished these potatoes your father and I will leave you in peace,' Mary said briskly as she glanced at her son. 'We'll be back about nine in the morning if that's not too early? That little parish church at the end of the street has a Christmas Day service at ten and I'd like to go, but of course you don't have to come if you'd rather not.'

The last few words had been directed at Candy, and her voice was somewhat vacant as she said, 'That would be lovely...' They would be back? Didn't that mean they had to go in the first place? What was happening here? 'But I don't understand—'

She stopped abruptly as she caught the quick shake of the head Quinn sent her as he looked pointedly from Candy to his mother bent over the potatoes.

What now? She frowned at him, thinking she had been *so* right when she had said she didn't trust him. If ever a man had his own agenda this one did.

Quinn continued to lean lazily against the door as they finished the vegetables, his conversation easy and amused as he teased his mother and made them both laugh, albeit reluctantly on Candy's part. It was only out of consideration for the feelings of Quinn's mother that she didn't speak out her misgivings, but as they finished the last of the potatoes and Mary began to wipe down the marble worktop Candy looked straight across at Quinn's dark face and said, 'I'll just pop down and say a quick hallo to the dogs, if that's all right?' knowing Quinn could do little else than accompany her.

'Yes, you do that, dear,' Mary said comfortably, 'and I'll be finished in here by the time the two of you return.'

'*Right, what is this, Quinn?*' Candy didn't wait until they were at the foot of the stairs outside the flat before she confronted him. 'What did your mother mean about coming back? Where are they going?'

'To the Saddler's Arms, as far as I know.'

'The Saddler's Arms?' They had reached the hall and she stared at him, her blue eyes narrowed in surprise. Ten o'clock on Christmas Eve and they were going out to the pub? 'For a drink?' she asked warily.

'I shouldn't be surprised. Dad always likes a Guinness or two before he goes to bed, says it helps him sleep,' Quinn returned congenially. Too congenially.

'So why can't he have a Guinness here?' she asked flatly.

'Oh, he could, he could.'

She'd hit him again in a minute!

Her face must have spoken for her, because the next moment Quinn took her arm and led her quickly through the big square hall, opening the door which led into the back of the building where the surgery kitchen, operating room and animal quarters were.

'Let go of me.' She shook him off once they were in the corridor beyond the hall and turned to face him again, her blue eyes shooting sparks. 'What's going on, Quinn? And don't prevaricate!'

'Nothing is "going on", as you put it,' Quinn said equably, 'it's just that the flat only has two bedrooms.'

'*What?*'

'So as the Saddler's Arms have their big double guest room free, and Mum and Dad decided they preferred that to the pad over the garages—although that's not a bad little place; I bunked down there for a time when I first came—'

'*Quinn!*' She never shouted; she wasn't the type of person who shouted. 'Are you telling me I've turned your parents out of their room?' she asked tightly, after a long hard breath.

'That's not the way I'd put it,' he said impassively, seemingly quite unmoved by her horror.

'Then how would you put it?' she snapped fiercely.

'I mentioned that lane of yours is a nightmare in bad weather; they agreed it was practical for you to come here if we could get them a room somewhere; we did… That's it,' he finished cheerfully. 'I don't think it even occurred to them that you might be happy to share my room after we've only been seeing each other for a couple of months,' he added with suspect reasonableness. 'They're a little old-fashioned that way.'

'I wouldn't be happy to share your room,' she shot back indignantly, 'of course I wouldn't. We aren't even *seeing* each other, not really.'

'Quite.' He smiled at her, a shark-like smile. 'So what's the problem?'

The problem was that she had suddenly found herself sharing a home with Quinn! And as problems went that was a mighty big one.

She stared at him, totally at a loss for words. He must realise? she asked herself silently. Even if he didn't want any involvement of even the most casual kind, he must understand that this wasn't fair on either of them? *Either of them?* The thought mocked her. You, you mean, her mind jibed nastily. Quinn is quite able to take you or leave you; he's proved that more than once. Whereas you…

Her chin rose a notch and her face straightened into cool, proud remoteness. 'The problem is exactly what I said before,' she said evenly. 'I don't want people thinking we are sleeping together when we are not.'

'Candy, the whole reason my parents have taken the room at the pub is because you are going to be in the guest bedroom,' Quinn said with insulting patience. '*That's* what people will think. If anyone has to worry about their reputation it's me, not you. My renown as a love 'em and leave 'em type is going to take a bit of hammering, don't you think? People will be expecting to hear wedding bells next,' he said with deprecating self-mockery.

She stared at him a moment more and then sighed irritably before she said, 'You've got an answer for everything, you know that, don't you?'

'Not everything.'

She was startled by the bitterness evident in his voice and for a moment she forgot the matter in hand and said urgently, 'Quinn, what's the matter?'

'You. You're the matter.'

It was the last answer, the very last answer she had expected, and her heavily lashed eyes opened wide with shock. 'Me?' she whispered faintly. 'What have I done?'

'What have you done?' He brushed an angry hand over his face in the same manner he used to rake back his hair, and the gesture told her he was truly thrown off balance. And angry. He was definitely angry.

And then she watched him gain control, and in that instant she knew, she just knew, as surely as black was black and white was white, that he had been playing a part ever since she had met him. She didn't exactly know *which* part, she admitted silently, but a part nevertheless. She had caught glimpses of the real man—brief, tantalising glimpses that had come and gone so quickly she hadn't been able to pin them down—but that was all. And a second or two ago had been one of them.

'You haven't done anything, Candy.' He was calm now, and very much Quinn Ellington, cool and self-assured man of the world, again. 'Come and say hallo to the dogs now you're here, and then we'd better get back upstairs; the parents'll be wanting to leave.'

He was just like Harper. One thing on the outside and quite another within. And then in the next moment she fiercely repudiated the thought. No, he wasn't like Harper—he wasn't remotely like Harper. Harper had been a vain, handsome, egotistical fraud, intent on taking the easy path through life whatever the cost to anyone else. And Quinn wasn't like that.

She didn't have time to think anything else. Quinn had opened the door to the surgery kitchen, where the dogs slept at night, and an avalanche of small furry bodies had poured out into the corridor in a frenzy of delight and wagging tails.

They spent some minutes with the dogs before Quinn shooed the pack into the long walled garden that was now several inches deep in snow. The lot of them went madly leaping into the new exciting white stuff that had transformed their playground, and immediately began a wild game of tag that had them jumping like gazelles and careering around as though they had springs on their paws.

'Crazy kids.' Quinn stood watching them for a moment, his hands thrust into the pockets of his jeans and his mouth twisted in an indulgent smile. 'We'll leave them to tire themselves out for a while.'

'Quinn, I'd really prefer your parents to stay here and me to go to the Saddler's Arms, or even the rooms above the garage,' Candy said quickly before she lost the opportunity as he shut the back door.

'I wouldn't.' His voice was faintly husky as he looked down into her earnest face, the dim light from the sixty-watt bulb in the corridor giving her eyes the look of deep midnight-blue pools and picking out shafts of gleaming copper in her luxuriant hair.

'But—'

'No buts.' He touched her half-open lips with a light finger. 'And you're not going back to the cottage either, before you suggest it. It's a sight too remote at the best of times, but with the prediction of the worst weather we've had for years…'

'It's not remote, not really.' He was too close, much too

close, and she was finding it difficult to be the impersonal friend he demanded in the very limited space within the corridor. 'Essie lived there by herself,' she added a little breathlessly.

'You're not Essie.'

It could have been insulting or demeaning or unflattering, but it was none of those things. The air was fairly crackling between them and his voice had been soft and deep with a warmth that made her feel deliciously cared for and hopelessly confused.

Quinn was breathing hard, his big muscled chest rising and falling beneath its covering of charcoal silk and his long lean legs slightly apart as he reached out and drew her into him. 'I want you to stay, all right?' he said thickly as he stroked her hair in an absent-minded caress, letting the smooth, silken strands run through his fingers as he looked down into her uplifted face.

His thighs were hard against hers, and with a little shock of pleasure she realised his body was betraying his desire. He moved, pressing her back against the wall of the corridor, holding her there with his body as he bent his mouth to hers.

And she welcomed his kiss, wanted it, her lips immediately opening beneath his and allowing him the intimacy he demanded with his probing tongue.

It couldn't be real, this heady sense of ecstasy that overcame her every time he touched her like this, she told herself helplessly. But it was. Every nerve, every sinew, the very blood pounding through her veins was reacting to Quinn's touch, and it was exhilarating and so, so sweet.

His hands left the rich silky tangle of her hair and moved down her body, roaming over the soft swell of her breasts, her waist, her hips. She could feel herself beginning to tremble but she couldn't control the quivering, and then his tongue rippled along her small white teeth, causing her to arch shudderingly against him as her hands on his shoulders pulled him closer.

Her breasts felt lush and full and there was a heat in the core of her she couldn't deny; suddenly all her intimate parts were on fire under his passionate touch and she wanted more, much more.

'Hell, Candy, what are you doing to me...?' It was a ragged whisper, but thrilling, and his rigid body was trembling almost as much as hers.

And then they both heard it; the careful call of his name from the hall beyond the corridor.

'Quinn, your parents...'

For a moment she thought he wasn't going to stop, and in spite of the fact the door might open any moment she wasn't at all sure that she wanted him to.

And then he drew in a long, shuddering breath, his chest rising and falling under the charcoal silk as he fought for control. He drew away slowly, his body leaving hers first as his hands left her soft voluptuousness and moved either side of her shoulders to the wall, where he levered himself off her with his mouth still stroking her lips.

'You want me as much as I want you.' It was a statement, not a question, and Candy could only stare at him as her mind raced madly. Yes, she wanted him, but just wanting him wasn't enough, not for her.

In the year or so since Harper had died she felt she had lived a lifetime, and not just because of the physical recovery that had been so slow at first. It was the mental scars that had been the hardest to overcome. Perhaps if she had been someone else, with no emotional baggage from her childhood and teens, Harper's betrayal wouldn't have hit her quite so hard. Perhaps. She would never know one way or the other about that.

But she *was* herself, warts and all, and she couldn't alter that. She was attracted to Quinn, more physically attracted than she had ever been to Harper, or any other man for that matter, but more than that she liked him too. She liked him very much. He had got under her skin somehow with his enigmatic personality—one moment so caring and gentle with his patients and anything small and helpless, and the next so remote and cool and controlled. He fascinated her, he annoyed and irritated her, he delighted her, and he made her feel more alive than she would have dreamt it was possible to feel.

And it was because of all that that she knew it would be sheer emotional suicide to start an affair with him. She simply wouldn't survive it when he decided to walk away. As he had already told her he would.

She expelled a quiet breath and then said the hardest sentence of her life. 'We can't always have what we want, Quinn.' And they both knew she was saying far more than the actual words.

He nodded slowly, his eyes on her flushed face. 'How did I know you were going to say something like that?' he drawled lazily.

But he didn't fool her this time. He was acting again, hiding the real Quinn under the easy, cool mask he liked to adopt when it suited him. She felt a sudden stirring of anger, and it propelled her down the corridor towards the far door with a regality that wasn't lost on the man looking after her. 'Your parents are obviously ready to go,' she said coldly over her shoulder, 'and it's rude to keep them waiting.'

The mental oath was never voiced, but Quinn's eyes were flint-hard as he followed her. Stop this now, a grim inner voice was warning him implacably. You know what you want for the future; you've got it all mapped out and you've made your decisions. There are a hundred women out there who can satisfy the physical side of things and none of them with any strings attached. Keep it distant, stay in control, watch yourself.

After the ruthless masculine beauty of the rest of the apartment, the guest bedroom was a surprise.

Once Candy and Quinn had said goodbye to his parents and gone upstairs, Quinn led her straight to her room, opening the door next to the master bedroom as he said, 'The bathroom's next door I'm afraid, but it's basically yours; I've got my own *en suite*.

'What a lovely room.' She had barely spoken since they had left the back of the house, but now there was a note of real delight in her voice.

The ceiling followed the roofline over the big double bed with an exquisite antique brass bedstead, and the room was simply furnished with a small wardrobe and a striking Queen Anne chest which the stained floorboards exactly matched. The dark wood and brass was the only contrast in the all-cream room, but there was decoration in the form of the beautifully embroidered bedlinen trimmed with lace and the enormous vase of pale, rose-touched lilies in the far corner of the room.

'Thank you.' He didn't tell her this was the one room which had been naked and bare when he had moved in, apart from the same silver-grey carpet which covered the rest of the flat. He had had that ripped up and had furnished this room in his own taste which, if he was being truthful, was more inclined to the rustic and antique than Essie's husband's had been.

'I feel guilty about those.' Candy was trying to bring a light note into the atmosphere, which had been strained, to say the least, since the incident in the corridor, as she pointed to the vase of flowers. 'You'd bought them for your parents and now they won't see them.'

Quinn shrugged easily. 'There'll be other times.'

'Yes, of course.' She tried to make her voice as relaxed as his but it was difficult. His dark masculinity seemed even more pronounced in the pale cream room, and since his hair had grown a little it was getting its tousled look back, which was so much more Quinn, somehow, than the cropped severity of the last few weeks.

'I'll leave you to unpack. Come through when you've finished and say goodnight to the cats,' he said coolly as the sound of Christmas carols from the TV drifted into the room.

She nodded, wondering why she wanted to cry. 'I'll do that.'

When she opened her case it took only moments to put her things away, and once that was done she stared down at the presents which had been under her clothes. Tabitha and the kittens each had a new toy, which she had wrapped in bright Mickey Mouse Christmas paper and was looking forward to seeing them rip open, and she had bought Quinn a small gift too. Of course that had been before she'd known she would be staying in his apartment, she reflected silently, as she thought about the heavy brass keyring in the shape of a bull—after the story about his battle with the bullock she had bought it a week or so ago—along with an expensive black leather wallet.

She hadn't anything for his parents. She sat down on the bed with a little plop. And she had seen a little pile of presents next to the Christmas-card tree. But there wouldn't be anything for her from his parents, she reassured herself in the next moment. They had been taken by surprise as much as she had. Or had they? She frowned. How long ago had Quinn told them he had a new 'girlfriend'?

She gathered up the parcels and hurried out of the room as doubt assailed her, walking into the sitting room to see Quinn setting a small table in front of the fire with two glasses of hot mulled wine and a small plate of mince pies.

'It *is* Christmas Eve,' he said almost apologetically, 'so I thought we should finish the evening on something of a festive air.'

'Right.' A small prickly sensation ran up and down her spine as she glanced at the two-seater settee in front of which he had placed the occasional table, but she put her unease to one side for a moment as she said, 'Quinn, I didn't know your parents would be here so I haven't bought them anything.' She nodded at the parcels in her hands. 'They haven't...?'

The black eyes flickered briefly.

'They have, haven't they?' she pronounced, horror-stricken. 'Oh, *Quinn*!'

'Don't panic,' he said soothingly. 'As you said earlier, I think of everything.'

She thought she had said he had an answer for everything, and she had not meant it to be laudatory, but now was not the time to split hairs.

'All you have to do is sign your name with your own flourish on their gifts,' he said smoothly, 'okay? Everything is ready for you to write the little cards. Here—' he walked across and picked up two parcels and brought them over to her '—I'll just get a pen.'

'What are they?' she asked suspiciously as she glanced down at the beautifully wrapped perfume-sized packages in her hands.

'Chanel No. 5, my mother has worn nothing else since she was a young girl, and Ralph Lauren for my father. He'll like it, I assure you.'

'Thank you.' It was grudging. Somehow here she was, giving his parents Christmas presents and spending the next couple of days in Quinn's guest room, none of which had been on the cards first thing that morning. What she had first thought of as a simple one-night piece of pretence to get Quinn off the hook with the local *femme fatale* some weeks ago had turned into a tangle with more threads than the average spider's web.

After something of a fight she persuaded Quinn to accept payment for the perfumes, and after she had written the little cards attached to the presents— 'The shop wrapped them, not me,' Quinn admitted cheerfully—she placed them next to the other parcels.

'Here.' As she turned from the cardboard tree Quinn patted the space beside him on the settee. 'Come and relax a while and put your feet up; Christmas starts right now.'

His handsome and slightly cynical face was trying to look innocent but she would as soon have trusted a cobra.

She stared at him before kneeling down on the rug in front of the gas fire next to the kittens, who were playing with rapt enjoyment with a woollen pom-pom she had made for them some days earlier, and holding out her hands to the heat. 'I'll have mine here, please.'

She turned as she spoke, holding out her hand for the glass of wine, but Quinn was already in the process of joining her on the rug. 'Good idea.' His voice was lazy and amused, and it stroked over her taut nerves with unbearable sensuality.

Candy took a big gulp of the wine before she realized the effect of its hot potency. There followed a brief but intense battle not to gasp and choke in front of him, but her eyes were watering as she fought for control. It was some moments before she felt sufficiently composed to turn her head and look Quinn's way, and then she wished she hadn't.

He was smiling, the hard lines of his handsome face mellowed in the attractive rosy glow from the fire and the lamp at the other side of the room. 'Got quite a kick, hasn't it?' he said in a tone of deep satisfaction. 'Have a mince pie.'

She didn't want a mince pie. She glanced at his big lean

body stretched out in comfortable indolence—and in stark contrast to her tense frame—as she acknowledged what she wanted definitely couldn't be voiced.

'No, thanks,' she said tightly. Why did he have to prop himself on one elbow like that? It seemed to emphasise his aura of raw masculinity a million-fold, and he was far too close again.

He shrugged, reaching for one of the pies on the plate next to him and biting into it with strong white teeth. 'Delicious,' he pronounced appreciatively, 'which is just as well. With the amount of these Marion has made added to my mother's stock I'll be eating mince pies at Easter. Philippa insisted on baking me a couple of dozen too. Do I look that hungry?'

Candy bit back the hot retort which had sprung to her lips on the lines of doubting whether it was feelings of benevolence which had prompted the beautiful blonde's generosity, and smiled sweetly instead. 'Not to me,' she said coolly. She hoped he choked on the rotten pie! And then she couldn't resist adding stuffily, 'Not that I've particularly noticed one way or the other.'

The black eyes were dancing. 'No, of course not,' he agreed soothingly.

There were a few moments' silence, which only the faint hiss of the gas fire and the kittens' mad scramble after the pom-pom broke, and then Quinn said softly, 'I didn't know girls still had freckles till I met you.'

'What?' Candy had just been wondering how soon she could drain the glass of wine and rise to her feet with a casual comment about going to her room, and now she cleared her dry throat as she said, 'Lots of girls just cover them with foundation, that's all, but there are thousands of women who don't.'

'Really?' he murmured huskily. 'Perhaps I just haven't been looking.'

Now *that* she did doubt!

'They're very…sexy anyway.' And then as her eyes shot to meet his he raised his eyebrows and added, 'What's the matter? Aren't I allowed to notice that?'

She wasn't sure just what little game he was playing, but it was dangerous without a doubt. 'You're allowed to notice anything you like, Quinn,' she said quietly, but with an edge. 'You're a free agent after all. And now, if you'll excuse me, I'm tired and I'd like to go to bed.' She finished the wine in two gulps, warning herself fiercely not to splutter as it burnt a trail down her throat.

'Me too.' His voice had a smoky tinge as he watched her rise gracefully to her feet.

'I'll put the cat basket in the recess in the kitchen, shall I?' she asked sternly, absolutely refusing to dwell on the connotations of the softly drawled words.

'Don't worry, I'll do it.' Quinn shifted position slightly and every nerve in her body responded. 'I might have another glass of wine before I turn in.'

'Right.' She stood looking down at him and felt faintly ridiculous when she realised she didn't know what to say. 'Well, thank you for having us all,' she managed lightly, the flick of her hand encompassing Tabitha and the kittens, the former watching her son crawl belly-fashion across the carpet as he stalked his two sisters, who had momentary control of the messy sphere of wool.

'My pleasure.'

The smoky flavour was stronger, and she could feel his eyes on the back of her neck as she walked towards the door.

'Candy?'

She actually had her hand on the doorhandle when he spoke and she had to nerve herself to turn and face him with a studiously blank expression. 'Yes?'

'Happy Christmas.'

CHAPTER SEVEN

When Candy awoke early on Christmas Day in the beautiful cream bedroom, she would have laughed in derision if someone had told her she was about to enjoy the best Christmas of her life. But from the moment she joined Quinn at the breakfast table an hour later there was magic in the air.

Quinn had metamorphosised into the perfect host; amusing, considerate, charming and attentive. And once Mary and Bernard joined them and the four of them had swapped presents the festive atmosphere just continued to grow.

Candy experienced a slight hiccup in her state of euphoria when she unwrapped Quinn's present to her. If she had expected anything at all it had been perfume, or something relatively impersonal, but the exquisite gold bracelet made up of tiny beautifully fashioned links which on closer inspection turned out to be minute cats, was anything but that.

'It's beautiful.' She raised surprised and wary eyes as her face flushed a rosy pink.

'So are you.' His hands cupped her face and he kissed her swiftly on the lips as his parents looked on approvingly.

Candy reminded herself, strongly, that they were supposed to be in the first throes of mad, passionate love, and managed to force a weak smile as she lowered her gaze to the bracelet in her hands. She hoped his parents would assume her lack of response to his kiss was embarrassment, as she had only known them for such a short time, and it appeared this was so as Mary said warmly, 'I have to say you are such a refreshing change from some of these rather hard-boiled types that seemed to be all the fashion these days, Candy. I'm not an anti-feminist, far from it, but so many girls seem to have lost the air of delicacy that makes women attractive, don't you think? And Quinn tells us you are a *wonderful* cook.'

'I wouldn't say that.' She raised her eyes to Mary's happy, smiling face and wondered what Quinn's mother would think if she voiced exactly what she was thinking right at this moment about her precious son! It wasn't fair to get Mary's hopes up like this, it really wasn't, not when there wasn't a chance of a relationship developing.

'Oh, but I would, darling.' Quinn was still standing next to her, and as she raised narrowed blue eyes to his handsome, satisfied face he must have read the very definite warning the azure gaze was sending, because his easy grin wavered a little and he quickly said, 'Here, let me put it on for you. The safety clasp is difficult to get used to at first.'

His hands were very big and strong as he took her slender wrist and draped the fine lacy bracelet over her skin, his fingers warm and sure of themselves. He stroked one thumb across the tender base of her hand before he let go, and she felt the mild caress like an electric current.

'Thank you.' She almost snatched her hand away; Mary and Bernard had turned away to rescue Alfie, who had managed to jam himself under the sofa as he hunted a scrap of Christmas paper, so there was no need to pretend.

If Quinn noticed the action he didn't betray it by so much as the flicker of an eyelid, and once they had finished the giving and receiving the four of them put on their coats and trudged through the snow, which was a good few inches thick, to the little church Mary had spotted the day before.

Quinn tucked her arm through his as they began to walk, pulling her into his side and looking down at her with such a deliciously sexy smile that it took every inch of the short stroll for Candy to pull herself together. But she managed it—just—and she had to admit, as she slipped into bed at the end of what had been a perfect day, that he had behaved faultlessly throughout.

Once the short service in the quaint fifteenth-century parish church had been over they had all wandered back to the apartment through the Christmas-card wonderland as a few lazy snowflakes had begun to fall, enjoying a couple of sherries before their enormous Christmas dinner of turkey and all the trimmings.

Candy and Quinn had taken the dogs for a walk in the silver glow of the afternoon—his parents had chosen to listen to the Queen's speech on TV before dozing in front of the fire—and then they had all tucked into turkey sandwiches, hot muffins oozing with butter and jam and enormous slabs of Mary's scrumptious Christmas cake before playing cards.

Boxing Day followed equally enjoyable lines, but then just after tea—when Mary and Bernard were due to leave to drive back to Oxford—Quinn's mother took Candy aside while the two men finished watching an action film on TV.

'Candy, I'm probably speaking out of turn,' Mary began quietly, 'but I just want you to know that this is the happiest I've seen Quinn in years. He is very fond of you, my dear.'

Candy stared at the older woman for a second as her brain refused to come up with coherent words, and then she stammered, 'We're more good friends than anything,' as she felt the hot flood of colour that had started at her toes surge into her face.

'But that's marvellous, don't you see?' Mary responded fervently. 'To my knowledge Quinn has never had that with any other woman, even poor Laura,' she added as her voice dropped even lower. 'He has always been popular with the opposite sex, even as a little boy the girls would fight to have him to their parties and make any excuse to call and see him, and he grew up thinking... Well...'

Quinn's mother suddenly looked extremely uncomfortable.

'That he only had to crook his little finger and they came running?' Candy put in somewhat dryly.

'Exactly.' Mary's tone was rueful. 'He never seemed to go through the spotty, gangly stage that afflicted most of his friends.'

No, she had to admit she couldn't see Quinn Ellington with pimples and awkward lanky limbs, Candy agreed silently.

'When he went away to university and then veterinary school he broke quite a few hearts,' Mary continued fondly, 'and then his paternal grandfather died and left him all he owned. Do you know about that?'

'No, no, I don't.' This was awful, terrible, but she didn't know how to stop the conversation from progressing unless she was rude, and she couldn't be like that with Quinn's mother.

'It was a considerable amount of money,' Mary said quietly, 'so now of course he had the added allure of wealth besides everything else, which is not particularly good at the tender age of twenty-six. I think he was what the younger generation call a "hellraiser" for a time, and then…he married Laura four and a half years ago.'

Candy shifted uncomfortably, and Mary suddenly seemed to be aware that she was talking too much. She patted Candy's arm lightly, her voice still confidential as she said, 'Well, anyway, my dear, suffice to say I have never seen him rush out to buy anyone flowers like he did on Christmas Eve when he thought you might be staying.'

Those flowers, the beautiful, exquisitely delicate lilies, had been specially for her? Candy stared into the warm, lovely face of Quinn's mother but she couldn't think of a thing to say.

'But now we really must be going.' Mary seemed unaware of the slight gape to Candy's mouth as she smiled brightly and called to her husband across the room, 'Bernard? We mustn't leave it too late, dear. The roads still might be difficult in places.'

Candy gave the impression she was carefree and breezy through the goodbye hugs and promises of future meetings, but once they had waved Quinn's parents off she took a couple of deep breaths. She was going to tell him she wanted to go home now, tonight, and she wasn't going to take no for an answer, she told herself resolutely. But then, as the tail-lights disappeared and the noise of the engine faded, Quinn quite took the wind out of her sails.

'Right, get your glad-rags on.'

'What?' They were standing on the top step, Quinn's arm casually round her shoulders, and now she shrugged him away as she said, 'What are you talking about?'

'Monty's party tonight,' Quinn said evenly and then, as though her abrupt tone hadn't registered, he continued conversationally, 'Always seems funny when I speak of Monty Hardingstone. I've a patient, a Great Dane, with the name of Monty, who has the devil of a time with his anal glands, and I can't help connecting the two in my mind.'

'Really.' Candy eyed him coldly, her tone indicating a hundred Montys—complete with anal glands or without them—were of no interest. 'You haven't mentioned this party before.'

'No?' Quinn raised surprised eyebrows in an innocent face.

'No. Which is a shame.' Candy smiled sweetly. 'Because it might have been fun. As it is, I really do have to get home,' she said with grim reasonableness.

'Why?'

'Lots of reasons.' She was *not* going to let him force her to justify herself!

'Name one.'

Because something had subtly shifted with his parents going, and she didn't want to explore what it was unless there was a good mile or so between her and Quinn! 'I shouldn't have to. I want to go home and that is sufficient,' Candy said with icy dignity.

'Not for me.' And he had the nerve to grin widely.

'*Quinn!*' Damn! She had promised herself she wouldn't lose control. 'I mean it.'

'Candy, it's gone six o'clock and that lane is as black as pitch at the best of times,' Quinn said mildly. 'I have absolutely no intention of battling down there when I can't even see clearly; that would be stupid.'

No, she was the stupid one—to think that she could trust a word Quinn Ellington said!

'I'll take you home in the morning, if you insist,' he continued steadily, 'but tonight we are going to Monty's party together, as planned.'

'It wasn't planned, not as far as I was concerned at least,' Candy said sulkily.

'Have you really had such a terrible time that you can't wait to leave?' he asked with sudden sad reproach. 'I thought it was a great Christmas.'

'It was. I mean—it was very nice. Your parents are very nice people.' Her voice trailed to a halt and she sighed deeply. Why did he always make her feel so *confused* she asked herself silently.

'So, Christmas was nice, my parents are nice, and what about me?' he asked with silky softness, his eyes brimming with laughter but his face quite serious. 'How would you describe me?'

'You don't want to know,' she shot back sharply, suddenly hurt in spite of herself. This was just a game to him, it hadn't touched his heart at all, whereas she...

The world stopped spinning and shot off into space as time splintered into a million tiny pieces.

She loved him.

Somehow, at some point in the last few weeks when they had been playing that insane game, she had committed the ultimate crime and fallen in love with Quinn Ellington.

It made all the other mistakes she had ever made—including her unquestioning blind devotion to Harper—pale into insignificance. She was the most stupid person in all the world, in all the universe and beyond. Stupid, stupid, *stupid*.

Hadn't she learnt anything in the last long, painful fourteen months? she asked herself fiercely. How could she have made such a fundamental error?

'...in about an hour or so?'

'What?'

Candy came out of the abyss with a start to find her eyes had been glued on Quinn's dark face, but without seeing or hearing anything but the black morass of her thoughts.

'I asked you if you could be ready in an hour or so.' Quinn's voice had a steely note now. He obviously didn't appreciate a female daydreaming in his exalted presence, Candy thought bitterly, as Mary's words about the constant adoration he had received from the opposite sex stung painfully.

'I...I suppose so.' She swallowed hard. If he was determined not to take her home until the next day a party was a darn sight safer than a cosy night at home.

'Good.' If he was surprised at her sudden capitulation he didn't show it. 'We needn't stay to the bitter end,' he added smoothly, for all the world as though it was his ancient granny he was escorting. 'I can see you are a little tired.'

What did that mean? That she looked awful? Candy's back straightened as hot colour flooded into cheeks that shock had made creamy pale.

She'd show him.

* * *

And an hour later show him she did.

She had only brought one faintly partyish dress with her, on the vague off-chance that Quinn might have a few friends round, but the silk-mix short-sleeved mini-dress in ice-blue with silver edging round the low neckline and sleeves dressed up very nicely when teamed with strappy silver sandals and long silver earrings.

She spent some time on her hair, looping the thick copper strands in deliberate disarray on the top of her head and securing them with pretty silver flower grips, before setting to work on her face, stroking silver eyeshadow on to her eyelids and then applying several coats of mascara to her naturally thick, curly lashes until her eyes resembled deep midnight-blue pools. Sexy plum lipstick, a brush of colour on her cheeks and one or two cheeky little glittering stars scattered on the cream swell of her breasts and she looked ready enough to party, she told herself firmly as she surveyed herself in the mirror an hour later.

There was a brittle smile on her lips as she walked into Quinn's sitting room a minute or two later, and it remained stitched on her face as she surveyed him lounging on the sofa as he waited for her. He looked simply gorgeous, but then he always looked simply gorgeous. It was just that tonight he looked *especially* gorgeous, which meant she had to be even more careful than normal, she warned her treacherous heart, which was pounding so hard it hurt.

One more night and then she could bow gracefully out of his life without him ever knowing she had made the ultimate fool of herself—like every woman he came into contact with, she added with bitter exaggeration. And she would do it. Oh, yes, she would. Bad as the experience would be, the alternative—of remaining close to him and one day giving herself away—was too debasing to contemplate.

*   *   *

The party was in full swing by the time they reached Monty Hardingstone's big grand stone house, and almost the first person they saw as they crossed the gracious threshold was a beautifully coiffured Joanna in the sort of slinky black strapless and backless dress that left nothing to the imagination.

'Quinn, darling...' Joanna was in distinct vamp mode, but was lovely enough to carry it off perfectly, and, judging by the number of men gathered around her, Quinn was the only one who was oblivious to the cool ash-blonde's charms. 'You must be the last to arrive. Naughty boy!' She had made her way to their side as she spoke and now tapped Quinn on the chest lightly, her eyes flashing a message that was blatant. She utterly ignored Candy.

Quinn's mouth had tightened ominously at Joanna's overt rudeness to the woman at his side, but whatever cutting comment he had been about to make was lost as Monty spoke just behind them in the next moment, forcing them to turn and acknowledge their host.

That Joanna had decided it was all-out war was obvious, Candy thought ruefully, when the other woman moved smoothly to Quinn's side as they stood chatting with Monty. Joanna immediately clung to Quinn's free arm, making a cosy little quartet, and when Monty took Candy's elbow and suggested she might like a glass of champagne it seemed as though there was nothing else she could do but walk with him into the massive crowded drawing room, leaving Quinn and Joanna bringing up the rear.

It set the tone for the evening. In spite of Quinn's frosty attitude with the sensuous Joanna she was never from their side for more than a few minutes, and brazen in her pursuit. She had obviously heard that Candy was staying at Quinn's apartment, and just as obviously didn't intend to bow out quietly.

You had to admire her sheer tenacity and confidence in

her own desirability, Candy thought more than once as the hours raced by in a haze of conversation and dancing. Joanna clearly considered herself the best thing since sliced bread, and even the most direct of Quinn's sardonic and often sarcastically cutting remarks just seemed to go right over the lovely blonde's immaculate head. She really couldn't believe that she wouldn't manage to snare Quinn in the end.

And somehow Joanna's determination to refuse to accept Candy and Quinn as a couple had seemed to rub off on Monty too. The big, jolly and slightly dim country gent was making no bones about the fact that he found Candy attractive, in spite of Quinn's dark hostility and barbed remarks that increased as the evening progressed.

It came to a head—as it was bound to—just after midnight, when Candy returned to the drawing room after visiting the cloakroom and searched the throng—many of whom were dancing to the strains of an old pop song—for Quinn.

'All alone, m'dear?'

She just managed to stifle the groan of irritation as she heard Monty behind her and felt his damp hand on her arm as he turned her to face him.

'Care for a little dance with old Monty, then?' he asked her loudly, his red moist face looking as though it was ready to explode.

She had already danced with him a couple of times and had no wish to repeat the experience; the second time she had had her work cut out to keep his big thick hands from wandering. 'I'm looking for Quinn, actually,' she said with a polite smile. 'He was going to fetch two platefuls of that wonderful buffet you've provided.'

'You don't want to worry about Quinn, m'dear.' The heavily perspiring face moved closer to Candy's and

Monty's voice was loudly confidential when he said, 'Joanna's looking after him, if you know what I mean.'

'I don't think I do.'

'They've had a little thing going for months on the quiet,' Monty continued affably, not at all put out by Candy's cool tone. 'Joanna told me herself—confidentially, you know?' He tapped the side of his greasy nose as he winked at her. 'And she also let on you've been asking about me, so no need to be shy, m'dear. I'm all for the modern way of doing things. Bit of variety is the spice of life and all that, eh?'

He was suggesting she and Quinn swop partners for the night with himself and Joanna? Candy stared at the grinning, amiable face in front of her. It was completely without malice or bashfulness; Joanna had obviously led him to believe his suggestion would be welcomed with open arms. Or perhaps the ice-cool blonde hadn't intended Monty to be quite so bald in his approach? Whatever, she had to put him right, and quickly. And then she found she didn't have to.

'I'm afraid Joanna has been taking a walk in cloud-cuckoo-land again.' Quinn's voice was like a steel blade behind Monty, and as Monty turned Candy saw Quinn had Joanna at the side of him. The beautiful blonde's face was scarlet with rage. 'I've just put her straight on a few things, and while we're on the subject I'd like to make it clear that Joanna and I have never been an item, Monty. Okay?' Quinn gave a smile that wasn't a genuine smile at all. 'So Joanna is all yours. And Candy—' here Quinn deliberately allowed his eyes to stroke Candy's flushed face '—is all mine.'

'Oh, I see.' The warning in Quinn's voice was obvious even to Monty. 'Ticketyboo, old man. Ticketyboo.'

'And we believe in fidelity. Isn't that right, sweetheart?'

Quinn held her gaze, his black eyes glittering. 'Both now and later, when we're married.'

Candy heard Joanna's sudden intake of breath and Monty's confused, 'Married?' but she was struggling with her own set of emotions, the chief being one of furious outrage. How *dared* he take this ridiculous farce so far? she asked herself angrily. Posing as his girlfriend was bad enough, but to announce to all and sundry they were intending to make it permanent was going beyond the call of duty. He could think of some other way to ward off Joanna Embleton-White because she had had enough. More than enough!

'So...' Joanna's gaze held all the warmth of an arctic winter. 'Do we take it congratulations are in order?' the slim blonde asked tightly, looking straight at Candy.

Candy didn't know what to say, but she summoned up a fairly bright smile from somewhere and wished Quinn Ellington to a place that was very hot and very final. 'Nothing is decided yet,' she managed at last, 'so perhaps congratulations are presumptuous.'

'Nonsense, darling.' Quinn was going for the Oscar. 'I want that band of gold on your finger as soon as possible and you know it.' He turned his dark gaze on Monty as he drawled easily, 'Can you blame me?'

'Not at all,' Monty responded gallantly, with an uneasy glance at Joanna's white, tight-lipped face. 'Quite understandable, old man.'

'I think so,' Quinn agreed with silky aplomb. 'And now, if you'll excuse me, I want to make sure my fiancée has something to eat. I'm sure we'll catch up with you later.'

Candy was so *furious* she didn't trust herself to say a word, steadfastly keeping her mouth shut as Quinn led her across the room and out into the hall towards the dining room where the sumptuous buffet reposed. But Quinn didn't lead her into the high ceilinged, wood-panelled dining room, as she had expected; instead he suddenly pulled her through a door to their left and Candy found herself in a large, book-lined study as Quinn flicked on the light and shut the door behind them.

'Calm down and hear me out before you say anything.'

Candy's head shot up as Quinn spoke, her vivid blue eyes shooting sparks and her soft mouth straight and taut. 'Nothing, *nothing* you could say would excuse such total, absolute arrogance, Quinn,' she snapped vehemently. 'How you could have the effrontery, the *gall* to stand there and tell them we're going to be married is beyond me!'

He was standing with his back against the door, leaning in a casual pose with his arms folded across his chest and his handsome head slightly tilted as he surveyed her wild expression. 'I was completely out of line. I know it,' he admitted calmly.

'Do you?' She was so angry she could have spit. 'Big deal! Why I didn't tell them you are an out-and-out liar I really don't know. I should have.'

'You didn't let me down in front of Joanna and Monty and the rest of them who were close enough to eavesdrop because you aren't like that,' Quinn said with unforgivable composure.

'You think I'm a fool, is that it?' she shot back hotly.

'No, that is *not* it.' His hand had clamped on to her wrist as she had made to turn away from him, hurt beyond measure, and now he took her upper arms in his hands, his fingers biting into her flesh as she struggled to break free. 'That's the last thing I think you are.'

'I don't believe you.'

'Then I'll have to convince you, won't I?' He had seen the telltale glimmer of tears deep in the sapphire eyes and his voice had gentled accordingly. 'I think you're pretty terrific, if you want to know, and I don't see any reason why we can't make my declaration a reality. We get on well, we each have our separate careers, so we're not likely to tread on each other's toes or get bored, and I'd bet my life we'd be more than compatible sexually...if you wanted that to be part of the deal. Of course that could happen at your own pace, when you're ready.'

'I don't believe I'm hearing this.'

She was staring at him as though he had lost his mind, and maybe he had, Quinn thought soberly, but he had had enough of Monty and the like pawing her about as though she was like the rest of the butterfly types who flitted in and out of their social scene. He'd wanted to do murder half the night.

'Why?' he asked calmly. 'I'm expanding the practice and a wife would be very useful to me. Dinner parties, entertaining—it is all so much easier with a hostess, besides which I'm tired of the Joannas of this world and their demands. You've had more than enough of the so-called love element to last you a lifetime, and so have I. And I would make sure you don't lose out on the deal. I am financially independent due to investments and other business deals; we'd live well. I could build you a wonderful studio at the back of the house—'

'*Quinn!*' She interrupted him before he could say any more. 'Quinn, we don't love each other.' Or you don't love me, more to the point.

'Exactly.' He smiled at her as though she had agreed to this ridiculous proposal. 'That's why it would work so well, don't you see? I've done the love thing and it's a killer, as your experience with Harper must have told you. But why should the past prevent us from enjoying life in a partnership in the future? The benefits are numerous. Think about it. We can be happy together knowing there are no great expectations on the other party; we can have fun, help each other out; my name and the ring on your finger will protect you from the Monty creeps and we can be friends too.

Many couples go through life without that ingredient, Candy.'

She remembered what his mother had said and eyed him helplessly. She was the only woman he had ever had a friendship with. Surely that boded well? And then she caught the thought frantically, shocked that she was even considering such a crazy notion. She couldn't agree to marry Quinn. The mere idea was emotional suicide.

'It wouldn't work. You must know that,' she said with deliberate casualness. He mustn't guess what this conversation was doing to her; the way her pulse was racing and her heart was pounding.

'On the contrary, I think it would work very well.' His dark eyes ran over her face and the mass of silky red hair. 'Marriages of convenience have happened from the beginning of time, and it's on record that they are more successful than so-called love matches.'

'So that's what this is, a convenient proposal?' Candy said flatly.

'I guess.' His eyes narrowed and he drew her closer. 'But I would satisfy you, Candy, in every way. Have no doubts about that.'

She didn't! Her tongue touched her lower lip and the pounding of her heart increased. He was offering her marriage! *Quinn!* He didn't love her—he would probably run a mile if he guessed her true feelings for him—but the impossible, the unthinkable had happened and he had asked her to marry him. She would never have a chance like this again.

If she said no she would be committing herself to a life of aloneness; she knew that. She would never find another man like Quinn—he was unique. True, she would have her work and friends, but did she really want to grow old with just the cats for company? There were some career women who flitted from one affair to another without letting anything affect them too deeply, but she wasn't like that.

And if she said yes? The thumping of her heart made her feel faint. Then she would be at Quinn's side, close to him, sharing all the small, intimate things that no one else would have the right to share. Maybe he would grow to love her? With time? But if he didn't would she be able to stand remaining on the perimeter of his heart?

And then the decision was made for her when Quinn bent his head and kissed her hungrily, his thighs hard against hers and his mouth sensuous.

He took his time, his mouth exploring hers with exquisite finesse until she was liquid heat in his arms, but still his lovemaking was controlled and restrained as he slowly fed her desire.

She knew what he was doing, knew he was using his considerable sexual experience to persuade and manipulate her to his will, but it didn't make any difference. She was just like all the others, she admitted painfully. She couldn't resist him. He was all-male, enigmatic and fascinating and so, so sensual, and she would never meet another man who could make her feel like this with such little effort.

She drew on all her resources and tried one last time to remain above water. 'Don't.' She wrenched her mouth away from his as she spoke, her voice trembling. 'Quinn, you have to see that this is crazy. What if either of us fall in love with someone else, what then? And this is so cold-blooded—'

'I'm not cold, Candy.' He took one of her hands and deliberately carried it to a certain part of his anatomy which was rock-hard. 'Does that feel as though I'm cold?' he asked brusquely into her shocked eyes. 'I want you and I can make you want me, but, like I said, you can take all the time you need on the physical side of things.'

She would *need* about two seconds flat, she thought with

dark ruefulness. He only had to touch her and she was his, if he did but know it.

'And what if either of us meet someone else?' she persisted as she looked up into his handsome face. 'What then?'

'That won't happen so it isn't a relevant possibility,' Quinn said with magnificent arrogance. 'I shall make sure you have everything you need from me.'

Everything but love. For an awful moment she thought she had said it out loud, but the sound filling her ears was the thud thud of her racing heart. 'But you might fall in love,' she said shakily. 'There would be two in this marriage, remember.'

'No, I won't, Candy.' He drew her against him again, nuzzling the silk of her hair as he said over the top of her head, 'I have enough antibodies from the disease to guarantee that.'

'Laura?' she asked faintly against the hard wall of his chest.

'Laura,' he agreed after a moment's tense silence. And then he began to talk. 'From the first day I met Laura we were inseparable,' he said quietly, 'but it wasn't until later, much, much later, that I realised she had done all the running. She was a terribly jealous woman. No—' he shook his head abruptly '—it was more than that. She was obsessional, unbalanced about me, but I didn't understand how it was at first. I cared about her, very much, and she was beautiful and vivacious and alive—so alive. By the time I began to question the rows that would result if I so much as glanced or smiled at another female Laura was pregnant.'

'Quinn, you don't have to tell me this.'

'Shush.' He drew her close again as she tried to lean back and look up into his face, and only when she relaxed against his chest did he continue. 'We were married within the month and on our honeymoon she admitted she'd done it on purpose because she was scared of losing me. I didn't know how I felt—angry, I guess, guilty because I made her feel so insecure and unhappy, trapped. But I still loved her and I was determined the marriage would work.'

He sighed, a deep shudder that came from some dark place within. 'It got so I was careful never to touch or even look at another woman, not even friends I'd known for donkey's years. We stopped going out to dinner because of the scenes that would inevitably result when we got home again, but I kept telling myself when the baby was born she'd feel better. More confident again, reassured of her beauty and figure. She hated being pregnant, loathed every minute of it, although I kept telling her she was more beautiful than ever and I meant it.'

'And when the baby was born?' Candy asked softly, and this time he allowed her to move back in his arms. 'What then?' she pressed gently as she looked into his tortured face.

'It was a difficult birth, and at first everyone blamed that on her inability to bond with our son.' The words were being torn out of him now, wrenched up and ground out through clenched teeth. 'I wouldn't let myself believe she was jealous of him and my feeling for my own son, but as weeks and months went by she made all our lives into a living hell. I insisted she went to a doctor, a psychiatrist, but it didn't help, and it got so I was frightened to leave her alone with him when I was at work. I hired a nanny— a woman old enough to be my mother who looked like the back of a bus—but she left after a few weeks when Laura accused her of sleeping with me. We were on our third nanny when I got a phone call one day. Laura had attacked the woman, who was fifty-five and very happily married with a brood of children and grandchildren, because of our "affair".'

'Oh, Quinn.' She didn't know what to say to erase the agony on his face.

'The nanny had tried to stop Laura leaving with my son after she'd fended her off, but by the time I got home it was too late. According to the police Laura must have taken a bend too quickly, which caused her to go off the road into the river, but...I've always wondered.' He shut his eyes briefly, then opened them as he said, 'Anyway, she went through the wall of the bridge and into the water and drowned them both. Joe wasn't even twelve months old.'

She wanted to take his face in her hands and smother him with kisses. She wanted to tell him she would make it all right, that she would love him enough for both of them, that she would heal all the pain and misery if it took her the rest of her life. But instead she stood quietly looking up at him and took a deep breath. She was on the edge of a precipice and she was going to jump off. She might be borne up on the breath of the future and learn to soar and fly, or she might be dashed to pieces on the rocks of the past. She had no way of knowing, because the end result rested with the tall, devastatingly handsome man in front of her.

But what she did know was that there had never really been any question as to the nature of her reply. She loved him. It was as simple as that. And she was scared to death.

'So...' Quinn looked down at her with midnight-black eyes in which there wasn't a trace of the usual cynicism and hardness. 'If you marry me it will be the traditional "till death us do part". Is that a problem?'

She took another deep breath and leapt into space. 'No, that's not a problem,' she said in a surprisingly steady voice, and lifted her face for his kiss.

CHAPTER EIGHT

THE next few months were ones of hectic activity. When Quinn had placed the exquisite diamond and sapphire star on Candy's finger on New Year's Eve he'd made it clear he envisaged a spring wedding, but within the week her agent had confirmed a small exhibition of her work in London for the end of April.

She had expected Quinn to object to the timing when she told him the news, but he had merely nodded slowly, his eyes narrowing, and had drawled, 'Fine. Excellent opportunity for you to get established here now it's going to be your permanent home. We'll set the wedding date for the middle of May, and apart from your dress and so on you can leave all the arrangements to me and concentrate on the exhibition. Okay?'

'But it means I'm going to be working flat out to get ready in time. You do understand that?' she had said quietly.

'Of course.' His tone had been almost distant, as though the last thing that concerned him was the possibility that he wouldn't see much of her, and it had caused Candy's chin to rise a notch and her mouth to tighten.

Fine. If he didn't care about not seeing her she was blowed if she would care about not seeing him either! But of course it didn't work like that in practice.

She had expected, once they were officially engaged, that Quinn would assume it entitled him to full seduction rights, but if anything, on the one or two occasions their busy schedules allowed them to meet each week, he was more distant and controlled than he had been before the engagement.

It didn't seem to worry him at all that they were ships that passed in the night, but it caused Candy many sleepless nights of tossing and turning, especially if she had seen him that evening.

Candy knew, taking into account all she had revealed about her past and the way she had rejected his physical advances, that she ought to be appreciative of his restraint and command of his physical desire, but she wasn't.

If she could have convinced herself Quinn was struggling and finding it hard to withstand her appeal it might have been easier, but he seemed content with the friendly, practically platonic relationship they shared. And it was driving her bananas!

She wanted him. In every single way she wanted him, physically, mentally and emotionally, and more than that she wanted him to want her too. But as the weeks went by fierce pride came to her rescue and enabled her to erect some barriers—flimsy, but nevertheless barriers all the same—against her deepest needs. She found Quinn wasn't the only one who could hide behind a mask.

And the deadline of the exhibition proved a blessing. She ate, slept and breathed her art, and apart from one weekend in March, when she drove up to Oxford at Quinn's mother's invitation and the two women went shopping for Candy's wedding dress, she worked non-stop at her painting.

Spring came early, and by the time the exhibition was due the air was warm and scented with clouds of May blossom.

Quinn insisted on driving Candy up to London at the beginning of the exhibition week and stayed with her for a day or so until work commitments prevailed, and she was grateful for the way his presence eased her into the exacting, difficult but very successful few days.

Too grateful, she told herself once he had gone home and she realised how much she missed him. She couldn't afford to rely on Quinn for emotional support, or at least no more than she would any other friend. Independence, friendship coupled with self-reliance and autonomy—that was the arrangement.

By the end of the exhibition Candy had made some valuable contacts and sold a considerable amount of her work, as well as taking an important commission that would keep her busy until the end of the year. The whole exercise had been a triumph, but with the wedding looming and just seven days away she was more keyed up than ever.

So all in all it wasn't really surprising, when Xavier and Essie arrived a couple of days early in the middle of the week, that Candy burst into tears of relief and joy and a whole host of other mixed-up emotions at the sight of them on her doorstep.

Xavier reacted with typical manly bewilderment and fluster, but Essie ushered her into the cottage and sat with her on the sofa, hugging her, soothing her and generally picking up the role of surrogate mum which she had assumed after the accident. Once Candy had made inroads into a box of tissues and Xavier had bumbled about in the kitchen making them all a cup of tea, the three of them saw the funny side of it, or at least Candy thought Essie had. Until the two women went upstairs for Essie to have a preview of the dress.

'Okay, what's wrong?' There was no amusement on Essie's beautiful face as she contemplated her husband's niece. 'And don't give me the same line as downstairs, that you were just so pleased to see us and tense about the wedding. I know there's more.'

'Oh, Essie.' Candy was sitting with the ravishingly lovely dress in her hands, and now she looked down at the cream Thai silk on her lap—the sleeveless, pencil-slim design and classical cut moulded to her figure as though it had been specially made for her—and sighed loudly. 'It's all so complicated.'

'It usually is,' said Essie, with all the wisdom of her changed shape. The baby was due in seven weeks and she was *big*. 'Especially if a man's involved. And Quinn is quite a man.'

'Tell me about it.'

'No, you tell *me*,' Essie probed gently.

Her lonely childhood and troubled upbringing had not been conducive to making close friends, but Candy knew Essie's history—an abusive, violent stepfather followed by a disastrous love affair when the other woman had been at university—and she knew if anyone could understand the tangle she had got herself into Essie would.

'You won't tell Xavier?' she asked pleadingly.

'Not if you don't want me to.'

And so Candy found herself telling Essie how she had come to be marrying the man she loved knowing he couldn't return the emotion, and the look on Essie's face by the time she'd finished made Candy bite her lip hard to prevent herself crying all over Essie's pretty blouse again. 'Don't be too sympathetic, Essie,' Candy warned chokingly. 'I'm a bit hormonal at the moment.'

'I'm not surprised.' Essie was frowning now. 'And I'm amazed at Quinn; I thought better of him.'

'It's not his fault.' Quite why she was defending him she didn't know, Candy thought ruefully. 'He doesn't know I love him and he thinks this arrangement is as much for my benefit as his.'

'Huh!' Essie's grimace made her point of view clear.

'And I'll be all right, really. It was just seeing you both again.'

'You ought to call it off, Candy, *now*. Or at least tell him how you really feel,' Essie said worriedly.

'No.' It was immediate and definite, and they stared at each other for a long moment until Essie said, 'Oh, Candy...'

When Candy awoke on the morning of her wedding it was to a perfect May day. The sky was a cornflower-blue, the sun was sailing high and the heady scents from Essie's garden were already perfuming the bedroom with their intoxicating fragrance although it was only six o'clock.

Candy sat up in bed and hugged her knees as her stomach went haywire. This was it. This was really it. Essie and Mary would be arriving at eight—Essie and Xavier were staying in a nearby hotel and Quinn's parents had spent the night in Quinn's spare room—to help her get ready for the service at eleven, and by noon she would be Mrs Ellington. Butterflies with hob-nailed boots began to do a dance just under her ribcage.

Toast. Two slices of toast and a cup of coffee and she'd feel better.

She pushed back the duvet and padded downstairs in her nightie without bothering to pull on her robe. The cottage seemed dead and empty without the cats—they had been living at the practice for the last couple of days and had already established their supremacy over the dogs and laid down the ground rules for future co-existence—and for a moment a sense of panic and something akin to desolation flooded her. And then she saw the package by the front door.

'This is a wedding present for the most beautiful girl in the world,' Quinn had written in his strong, firm hand, 'and my future partner through life.' There was no signature or 'love', just a black 'Q' that ended in a flourish.

The pearl necklace and earrings were exquisite.

He must have walked down the lane and slid them through the letterbox when she was asleep, because she hadn't heard the car, Candy thought as she gazed at the smooth, lustrous pearls with a thudding heart. And 'the most beautiful girl in the world' was a start. Wasn't it?

And she was thinking just that, concentrating on the thought and that alone, as she walked down the aisle on Xavier's arm five hours later.

Her delicate dress flared out demurely over her satin pumps, the fragrant cream rosebuds entwined in her hair and tiny frothy veil surrounded her in a cloud of perfume and chiffon, and the rosebuds were reflected in the bouquet she carried, along with deep red roses and trailing freesias and fern.

Quinn turned to her as she reached his side and for a brief moment the mask was ripped aside and she saw the fierce hunger and dark desire he had been keeping at bay for so long. She stared at him, quite unable to smile for a moment as the unexpectedness of seeing his passion laid bare after his remote coolness of the preceding months brought her eyes wide with shock. Almost immediately the mask was back in place as he saw her expression, and the service was commencing.

And then she was walking back down the aisle, but this time as Mrs Ellington, her arm in Quinn's and his big lean body in its grey suit and cream shirt and cream and gold waistcoat at the side of her. He was her husband; she was his *wife*.

They emerged to the ringing of the church bells and brilliant sunshine, and as the photographer led them over to a cherry tree bordering the cobbled church path, its mass of ethereal blossom the perfect setting for the wedding photographs, Quinn smiled down at her as he touched the pearl necklace at her throat.

'It doesn't do such beauty justice,' he said softly, his voice low and deep. 'There isn't a man alive who isn't envying me right at this moment.'

'A slight exaggeration,' she managed breathlessly, her heart pounding. There was a dark power in his magnetic attractiveness at the best of times, but today the sensuous charm was overwhelming.

His ebony eyes held her azure-blue ones for a second, and then Quinn said, his voice a throaty murmur for her ears only, 'Don't be frightened of me, Candy. I meant what I said. You can take all the time in the world.'

He thought she was nervous of the night ahead? She stared at him, searching for the words to tell him he had it all wrong without giving her real feelings away, but her inexperience was against her and the moment to speak was lost as the photographer turned and began positioning them in the traditional wedding poses.

The rest of the day passed in a whirl of images and voices, none of which Candy felt she would remember. It was as though she was the chief performer in an elaborate play; none of it seemed real.

But it was real. *She was married. To Quinn.* It was his ring on her finger and his arms holding her close as they danced the evening away, and it was his bed she would sleep in from this night forth.

She missed her step at the thought and immediately his dark face peered down at her, his voice very deep as he said, 'Tired? It's been a long day.'

'Not really.' Tired? She was so keyed up with excitement and nervous anticipation that the adrenalin was pumping like a piston in every nerve and sinew, she thought a trifle feverishly. It probably wasn't at all the appropriate thing on a girl's wedding day, and it certainly negated that 'air of delicacy' that Quinn's mother had complimented her on at Christmas, but all she had been able to think of for the last few hours as she had floated in his arms was how he would make love to her once they were alone.

Quinn naked, that big, lean body in all its magnificence

stretched out next to hers. His hands and mouth on her skin, her breasts, her thighs, touching her, pleasuring her...

She missed her step again, and this time he stroked the back of her neck with soothing fingers that were unbearably erotic as they massaged tense muscles. 'Come on, time to slip away,' he said huskily. 'Let's make our goodbyes.'

Her heart was beating in her throat as she forced her legs to carry her overwrought self off the little dance floor at the hotel Quinn had booked for the reception and begin the round of farewells.

She was tucked into his side as though she belonged there, and it was wonderful.

When they came to Essie and Xavier, Essie's gentle, 'Candy, we wish you both all the happiness in the world,' made her swallow hard.

She was able to say, 'We'll be happy, Essie, I know it,' with a message in the words just for the other woman alone.

Essie looked hard and long at her, and whatever she read in Candy's face seemed to satisfy her, because she smiled gaily and murmured, 'Of course you will, darling.'

And then there was the mad flourish of their exit, when Candy threw her bouquet into the squealing crowd of eager women who had gathered to catch it, and they were outside in the warm May night and surveying Quinn's beautiful Aston Martin, which several bright sparks had covered in ribbons and shaving foam and risqué messages, as well as fixing to it a train of cans several feet long.

Quinn had offered her the choice of any place in the world for their honeymoon when they had set the wedding date, and when Candy had shyly asked if they could stay right where they were in England and tour round so that she could see her adopted country he had been quite amiable, if a little quizzical. 'Funny girl.' He had touched her hair lightly with a mocking hand. 'But if that's what you want...'

What she *wanted* was him, and now the same flood of whirling elation and thrilling warmth that had filled her that day at the thought of having Quinn all to herself for three whole weeks made her cheeks flush again.

She would *make* him love her, she told herself excitedly as Quinn settled her in the front of the car with careful attention to the shot-silk dress and jacket that was her going-away outfit. She would. It was a strange thought that she was setting out to seduce her own husband, but that was what it boiled down to, she supposed. Certainly the wildly sexy black lace thong pants and black lace bra she was wearing would cause any man to take a second look, especially when teamed with gossamer-thin stockings and suspender belt.

She had never worn a suspender belt before, and although it felt strange it made her feel sensual too, and very definitely a wicked woman. And that was what she wanted to be for Quinn. Mistress, wife, lover, friend... whatever he needed.

She had shocked herself at first, when she had realised she wanted to do to Quinn everything she had ever read lovers did and much more besides, and that she wanted him to do the same to her. It had caused her to wonder if she had more of her grandmother in her than she had suspected, until common sense had come to her aid.

She *loved* Quinn, completely, utterly and for ever—this wasn't some hole-and-corner affair that would be repeated with a different man once the present one grew tired of her. It made all the difference in the world. She took after her mother—not her grandmother.

As Candy saw Quinn's mother—her hands pressed to her chest and her eyes moist—from the passenger window, something in the other woman's face made her wind down the window and call to her. Mary must be remembering that other marriage, and all the pain it had entailed, and although she knew Quinn's mother liked her this wasn't an easy time for the older woman.

As Mary approached the car Candy opened the door and stood to her feet, hugging the other woman close for a few moments before she said softly, 'I'll look after him, Mary. I promise.'

'I know you will.' The tears were streaming now.

'And we won't be that far away,' Candy added comfortingly. 'Any time you want to come down for a few days you will be welcome. You know that, don't you?'

'Bless you, dear.'

'Did you mean that?' The shouts and cheers of their guests faded into the background and the night swallowed the car in its mellow blackness as Quinn drove swiftly along the road away from the hotel. 'About them coming to stay with us?'

'Of course.' Candy glanced at him in surprise, but Quinn kept his eyes on the dark country vista beyond the windscreen as he said, his voice almost expressionless, 'Thank you. That will mean a great deal to her. Laura...Laura never liked them to visit, you see. We only lived a short drive away in Oxford, but even after Joe was born Laura made any contact a trial by fire, and although I used to ask them just the same my mother wouldn't make things any more difficult for me than they were. I think she ached to see more of Joe, though.'

'I'm sorry, Quinn.' She was, terribly, but the mere words sounded inept and inane.

It was another few moments before Candy said quietly, 'Where are we staying tonight? Is it far?'

'Not too far.' He shot her a quick smile, but it was remote, almost polite. 'I thought a hotel was a little impersonal, especially as you're bound to be tired tomorrow and will probably want a late start, and it just so happens an old friend of mine is in the States at the moment and he offered his farmhouse for as long as we wanted it. We can relax there for a day or two and then start the grand tour, if that suits, Mrs Ellington?'

'Certainly, Mr Ellington.' She tried to inject her voice with the light, bantering tone he had used, but it was difficult with her heart thudding so hard it made her dizzy.

The 'farmhouse' turned out to be one of the most enchantingly beautiful homesteads Candy had ever seen. It was huge, with a bevy of mullioned windows twinkling under their mop of thatch and surrounded by acres and acres of grounds, set all by itself in the countryside.

Once Quinn had shepherded her inside she found the interior was the last word in old-worlde luxury; oak beams, gleaming brasses, deep sofas and cherrywood floors all reeking of unlimited wealth.

'What does your friend do for a living?' Candy asked breathlessly when she walked into the massive luxury kitchen that was fitted with every gadget under the sun but still retained a country charm, with bunches of dried flowers hanging from the ceiling and a superb farmhouse table and chairs in the middle of the terracotta-tiled floor.

Quinn shrugged easily as he walked over to an enormous fridge-freezer and extracted a bottle of chilled champagne. 'Stocks and shares,' he answered off-handedly. 'He's a financial wizard. Here, we'll have a glass of bubbly and then I'll show you the upstairs. It's gone twelve and you must be exhausted.'

Upstairs. She jumped a little as the champagne cork popped, and then blinked at him as he handed her one of the fluted glasses. *Upstairs*. All the hidden fantasies and forbidden sweet, erotic dreams were going to happen. She was going to lie in his arms; he was going to make love to her.

'To you, Mrs Ellington.' Quinn raised his glass as he

spoke, his ebony eyes unfathomable and his handsome face smiling.

'To us,' she corrected bravely, the blood pounding in her ears as she kept her gaze on the glittering eyes.

'To us.' He lightly touched her glass with his and then downed half the contents in one swallow before lowering his head, his gaze never leaving hers. His mouth was warm and tasted of champagne, and the alcohol's fizz seemed to have transported itself to her ears, which were buzzing.

His mouth parted her lips, slowly and sensuously, and as his tongue probed the hidden depths she had to will herself to stop the little moan that had started somewhere in the core of her. But she couldn't hide the shudder that her desire had caused. Immediately his mouth withdrew, as he mistook her reaction, and he turned, walking to the door before she could bring coherent words out of the turmoil of her mind and ask him to kiss her again.

'Come on, come and see the rest of it,' he said coolly, holding out a commanding hand as he turned to face her again in the open doorway.

He was so in control, so unaffected by her... She forced her shaking legs to totter over to him and took the hand he offered. But she had turned him on more than once in the past, she knew it, and she would do it again if it killed her.

The farmhouse staircase was more suited to a Hollywood movie than anything else, but as Candy climbed the huge winding and very gracious steps to the galleried landing above, she was quite oblivious to her surroundings.

What should she say when they went into their bedroom? she asked herself feverishly. Or perhaps she wouldn't need to say anything at all? When he started to make love to her again she would let her mouth and her hands speak for her. Quinn was a sensual, passionate man; his virility clothed him like a dark aura. He had already said he found her beautiful and sexy. It would be all right. *It would be all right.*

'There are the nursery quarters and two bedrooms on the second floor above,' Quinn drawled easily when they reached the landing, 'but they will wait until tomorrow. These are guest bedrooms, all with their own *en suite*—' he opened three doors in quick succession to show her massive bedrooms beautifully furnished and each with a separate colour scheme '—and this is the master bedroom.'

This time he indicated for Candy to precede him into the vast, high-ceilinged room, which was decorated in silver and a deep violet-blue, and she saw their holiday luggage—which she had assumed was in the Aston Martin—was all ready *in situ* and must have been brought over earlier in the day.

'What a truly incredible house,' Candy breathed softly as her eyes roamed the lovely room. 'Your friend's a very lucky man to have found a place like this.'

'He's thinking of selling it, actually.' Quinn was leaning against the open door, his arms folded across his chest and his dark eyes watching her. 'He spends most of his time in the States now, and his wife and children get tired of seeing him once in a blue moon.'

'Really?' She turned to face him. 'But who on earth would be able to afford somewhere like this?'

The black eyes were contemplative as he said lazily, his tone matter-of-fact, 'Me, actually. If you like the thought of living here permanently, that is. There's an indoor swimming pool built on in an annexe at the back of the kitchen and a pretty well-equipped gym. It would be no trouble to extend a little further and add a studio.'

'You could buy this place?' she asked, her voice high. And then, realising how rude her amazement sounded, she added hastily, 'What I mean is—'

'I know what you mean.' He didn't sound at all offended

'I was left some money, a large amount of money, when I was younger, and Matt, the guy who lives here, invested a substantial amount for me—very wisely, as it happens. It grew, I played the stock exchange now and again, with Matt's guidance, and perhaps perversely—because I didn't care much if I won or lost—everything I touched turned to gold.'

'But...' She stared at him, her lovely blue eyes puzzled. 'If you could afford somewhere like this why did you move in over the practice when you bought it? And why work as a vet at all?'

'To answer your last question first, I like it. I trained for it. It was tough, but I got through, and it satisfies something deep inside,' he said steadily.

She nodded slowly. Yes, she could understand that. If she made a billion tomorrow she would still paint.

'As to why I moved into the flat—why not?' He shrugged as he straightened up from the door. 'I was a bachelor again, and intending to remain so. When Laura and Joe died I went through a bad patch—' the hard mouth tightened '—and I dropped out of life for a time. You can do that when you've got money.' It was cynical and self-derisive, but before she could say anything he continued, 'And then I started working as a vet again and it was my salvation. I needed it. So in the back of my mind I began to think it might be good to get my own practice again, like I had in Oxford when I was married. I travelled around a bit in my spare time to see the sort of area I'd like to live in—I was tired of the big cities—and then I answered Essie's advertisement for a vet. The rest, as they say, is history.'

She stared at him. 'Why didn't you tell me you were so wealthy before?' she asked quietly, her even tone masking the hurt. He played all his cards so close to his chest; she really didn't know this man at all. But he wasn't just a man, was he? He was her husband.

'Does it matter?'

His voice was so calm it was an insult, and her heart began to beat erratically as she realised just how little he had revealed about himself during the time she had known him. Every time she thought she was getting the tiniest bit close he let her know she still had miles—a lifetime—to go.

'I think so, yes.' She raised her chin slightly but her eyes didn't flicker as she continued to stare into his. 'I know this marriage is one of convenience, but there has to be a foundation of trust at least,' she said levelly, wondering where the strength and control was coming from to speak so matter-of-factly when she was so churned up inside.

His eyes held hers for an infinitesimal moment longer, and then he jammed his hands into his pockets, the action showing her he wasn't so calm as he would like her to believe. 'Point taken.'

She hoped so, but she doubted it. He clearly envisaged they would be two people living under the same roof but engaging in separate lives. Well, that wasn't altogether his fault, but there was no time like the present to start chipping away at that formidable steel coating he had put on his emotions.

'Good.'

She managed a fairly normal smile, which froze as Quinn said, 'Is there anything you need before you turn in?'

It wasn't so much the words themselves but the way he had spoken—that and the fact that he was already stepping backwards into the hall, his hand on the door to pull it shut.

'Yes... No! I—' She stopped abruptly, trying to gather her scattered wits. He couldn't be saying what she suspected he was saying, could he?

He could.

'Try and get a good night's sleep; it's been an exhausting day,' Quinn said evenly, and then quietly closed the door, leaving her alone.

CHAPTER NINE

CANDY remained standing where she was for a good minute as she struggled to take in that her new husband—her brand-new husband—had abandoned her on their wedding night.

Then she walked over to the bed—a huge four-poster—and threw herself down on the antique lace coverlet and had a good cry. It helped—a little; at least it enabled her to strip off the erotic underwear with bitter mutterings along the lines of 'It's his loss, the rat,' and no more tears.

She padded into the *en suite* stark naked and found an amazing bathroom that would make even the most hard-boiled movie star sit up and take notice. All marble and mirrors and concealed lighting.

Candy spent some moments examining herself from all angles in the mirrored walls and ceilings. Okay, so she wasn't one of those stick insects that were in all the fashion magazines these days, but neither was she grossly fat either, she reassured the pink-eyed reflection dismally. She had had guys coming on to her from when she was barely in her teens, so she couldn't be *that* bad, could she?

She ran herself a bath in the sort of super-tub that would easily have accommodated a team of rugby players and flicked the switch to Jacuzzi mode, refusing to allow her mind to play on how different it could have been if Quinn were here at the side of her.

She hated him! She did, she loathed him, she told herself savagely. She wouldn't allow him within ten feet of her if he went down on his knees and begged! How she could have imagined she loved him she just didn't know; she must have been having some sort of brainstorm. But she was in her right senses now and she could be every inch as cool and controlled as he was.

He had said she could take all the time she needed to make their relationship a physical one and she would certainly do that all right. He would still be waiting when he was an old man with grey hair! He had shown her the matter was incidental as far as he was concerned, so there was no problem, was there? No problem at all.

This chain of thought was threatening to bring on the tears again, and so she determined to suppress all thoughts of Quinn and let the silky bubbles ease her stiff limbs and tense muscles.

She stayed in the water for over an hour—she would turn into a dried-out wrinkly prune and that would show Quinn, she thought with total irrationality—and then dried herself slowly, wrapping the huge fluffy bath sheet round her sarong-style before walking back into the bedroom. Its emptiness mocked her as she dried her hair and smoothed moisturiser into her face and body, but it was when she walked over to the luggage and realised there were only her two suitcases standing there that the tears surfaced again.

He really didn't want her. She sank down on the bed and gazed round the fabulous room vacantly. Or not enough, at least. Where was she going to find the strength to change things? *Could* she change things?

She suddenly felt very small and very alone—and unloved. Unloved and unlovable. It wasn't a new feeling; it had reared its head all through her somewhat isolated childhood in spite of Xavier's efforts to be all the family she needed. But tonight the feeling was overwhelming, and it emphasised her utter presumptuousness in imagining she could make Quinn Ellington fall in love with her. She must have been mad! She *was* mad—stark, staring crazy.

She rolled into a tight little ball under the crisp cotton covers and cried herself to sleep.

When Candy awoke the next morning it was out of a deep, dreamless sleep of mental, emotional and physical exhaustion. She surfaced slowly, layer upon layer of thick cotton-wool heaviness anchoring her to the bed, but then it dawned on her somnolent senses what had roused her. Someone had drawn back the thick violet-blue drapes and opened the windows, letting fresh golden sunlight spill into the room.

She opened her eyes to stare straight into Quinn's glittering black gaze.

'Come on, sleepyhead,' he said lazily, his dark eyes washing over her tumbled red hair and creamy skin as Candy instinctively pulled the bedclothes more closely around her. 'It's ten o'clock on a beautiful summer Sunday and we're going to explore Matt's magnificent grounds. I've packed a picnic lunch already, so once you've eaten your toast and drunk at least two cups of coffee we'll be off.' He indicated the breakfast tray he had placed on the small table at the side of the bed with a smile.

'You've got breakfast?' She remained exactly where she was, half snuggled under the covers, because she remembered she had been too miserable last night to search her suitcases for a nightie and had slept nude.

'It didn't need much getting,' he returned dryly, glancing at the tray containing a glass of fresh orange juice, three slices of buttered toast and a tiny pot of blackcurrant preserve, a jug of steaming coffee, sugar and milk, along with a china mug gaily painted with poppies. 'I'll give you half an hour, okay?'

'Okay.' She nodded obediently, silky tendrils of hair falling about her face and the blue of her eyes still smudged with sleep. She just wanted him to go! He looked gorgeous—freshly shaved, black hair still damp from the shower and dressed with immaculate casualness in an open-necked charcoal silk shirt and black jeans—whereas she must look a fright.

And then, almost as though he had read her mind, he bent down and took her flushed face in his hands, planting a swift kiss on her surprised lips before straightening again. 'I knew you'd look good enough to eat in the mornings,' he said over his shoulder as he strolled over to the half-open door. 'Half an hour, and don't keep me waiting.'

He knew she'd look good enough to eat? If he hadn't closed the door he would have got the tray aimed straight at the back of his arrogant head, coffee and all, Candy told herself furiously as she jerked into a sitting position. Talk about blowing hot and cold!

All these months of touch-me-not culminating in the fiasco of last night and he *dared* to imply— What, exactly? What had he implied? She sat there, her glorious hair spilling about her slender shoulders and her brow creased in a frown. That he fancied her? That he wanted her? But he might not have meant that, might he?

She glanced at the breakfast tray and sighed, loudly and irritably. Quinn Ellington was a law unto himself, that was the trouble, and if she was being absolutely honest she didn't have a clue what made the man tick.

The thick gold band next to her engagement ring felt alien and heavy on her hand as she reached for the breakfast tray and, after drinking the orange juice, nibbled at a slice of toast. She wasn't in the least bit hungry; she didn't feel as if she would ever be hungry again, she told herself miserably. And she had no one but herself to blame for this mess. Quinn hadn't forced her to marry him; she had gone into this with her eyes wide open. She just hadn't expected...

'Oh, quit griping!' She spoke the words out loud, her tone suddenly firm, and felt better for it. This was her first day as Mrs Quinn Ellington and she was blowed if she was going to spend it moping and whining. She was young, she was healthy, her career was about to take off in a big way and she was married to the man she loved. Admittedly he didn't love her, but who said life was ever perfect? She grimaced derisively to herself, finishing the slice of toast in two bites, and threw back the covers determinedly.

A picnic, he'd said. And exploring the grounds. She ought to wear something very practical, like jeans and a top, or shorts, maybe, but this wasn't a time for practicality. This was a time for making Quinn Ellington squirm! He was a man with a very healthy libido and she would make him pant on the leash if it was the last thing she did. And then she would—very politely but firmly—remind him of all he'd said and make him pant some more.

It took an extra ten minutes over the allotted half an hour to get ready, but when Candy stood surveying herself in the full-length bedroom mirror she told herself it was worth it. The white, full-skirted, sleeveless dress in fine broderie anglaise was ethereally lovely but subtly sexy too, with its plunging neckline and tightly fitting bodice ending in a deep V, and at least her white pumps were flat and easy to walk in. She closed her mind to the thought of grass stains and blessed the hot weather which had made everything tinder-dry.

She had curled her hair about her shoulders, where it hung in shining waves, and applied just enough eye make-up to turn her eyes into deep pools of sapphire without it being obvious she had made herself up. Her skin was glowing and smelt delicious, thanks to the horribly expensive body lotion she had used with gay abandon, and her pale peach lipstick gave her lips a moistness that would make any red-blooded man want to taste them.

She caught herself at the thought, staring at the image in the mirror with eyes that suddenly widened. What on earth was she doing? she asked herself faintly. What had Quinn turned her into? This wasn't the shy, nervous girl who had firmly repulsed all suitors most of her life and only allowed Harper the briefest of intimacies. She was behaving as brazenly as Joanna!

Galvanised into action, she scrubbed at her lips with a tissue, but got no further before she heard Quinn call from beyond the bedroom door. She had no time to change now. She glanced at her reflection and grabbed a scrunchy from her cosmetics bag, looping her hair high in a ponytail with the elasticated band and standing back to survey the effect. Better. Definitely not so come-hitherish.

The knock on the bedroom door had her springing across the room and opening the door to see Quinn leaning against the far wall, his hands in his pockets and his dark eyes slumberous as they travelled over her hot face. 'All ready?'

'Uh-huh.' Ready? She had never felt so less ready in all her life, especially when confronted with the pure male sensuality that was an intrinsic part of Quinn and lethal in content. She forced a quick smile and pulled the door shut behind her as he levered himself off the wall and held out his hand. Help! Double help! *Triple* help! She took his hand and walked with him down the stairs and out into the sunshine, as though the feel of his warm fingers holding hers wasn't causing her heart to beat in her throat.

Quinn stopped just outside the threshold of the house, locking the door before picking up the wicker basket at the side of the stone steps. 'Lunch,' he explained briefly, and then handed her a pretty little homemade corsage of bright white daisies with gold centres. 'I had to fill in the time while I was waiting,' he said lazily in reply to her delighted thank you.

'Here.' He took the flowers from her and fixed them into the band holding the ponytail. 'Perfect.' He stood back to admire the effect and then, as she smiled at him, the laughter died in his eyes and was replaced by something much more raw before he bent and picked up the basket again.

'Matt tells me there are some fifty acres of grounds in all,' Quinn said quietly as he reached for her hand again and drew her further into the sunshine. 'Formal gardens surrounding the house, then the orchards and paddocks beyond, and beyond them he's let a good number of acres grow into wild meadow. His wife is something of a conservationist,' he added almost apologetically. 'She's into planting wildflowers and so on.'

'Good for her.' Candy glanced at him, so big and dark at her side, and felt her heart turn over. 'I love wildflowers; they're the prettiest of all.'

'Yes, I thought you might.' He glanced at her, the black eyes narrowed in a face that was too handsome by half. 'We'll just follow our noses, then?'

Unlike her wedding day, Candy was to remember every minute of that wonderful day for the rest of her life. There was a slight breeze in the air which stopped the day from being too hot, and as they strolled along in the warm sunshine they talked easily—too easily, Candy was to think later, when she realised just how much she had revealed about her childhood hopes and fears and the way things had been—until, just after two, when they were knee-deep in the meadows Quinn had spoken of, he suggested they eat lunch.

'What a wonderful, wonderful place.'

The grassy dell in which they were sitting was a carpet of wildflowers, their scents perfuming the still summer air and causing the steady drone of bees to become a low background hum as they searched for pollen.

'Step out of life,' Quinn agreed lazily, and then, as he unpacked the very superior picnic hamper and caught her amazed eyes, he grinned, adding, 'Courtesy of a first-class local delicatessen, I'm afraid. I'd like to take the credit but my innate honesty forbids it.'

It was the grin that did it. It was beguiling little boy and sexy man of the world and a million other things besides, and yet another facet to Quinn's complex personality. She *knew* there were countless other women who would be bowled over, just as she was, but it didn't make any difference. He was devastating. Devastating and dangerous and frighteningly irresistible.

But she had to resist him. Candy tried to summon up the antagonistic spirit of earlier but it was hopeless. Then she had been alone in her bedroom—now she was with Quinn, the real flesh and blood man, and it made all the difference in the world.

'Here.' He handed her an elegant crystal glass filled with deep red wine, which was as far removed from the paper cups and warm lemonade Candy associated with picnics as chalk from cheese, and raised his own glass as he said, 'Another toast, from you this time?'

There were a hundred and one things that sprang to mind, but all of them would have destroyed the carefree mood of the moment, and so she dismissed terms like 'lifelong happiness' and 'our future together' and said instead, her mouth smiling, 'To more picnics like this,' and was rewarded by his appreciative chuckle.

The wine tasted of cherries and blackcurrants and hot summer days in the country and made her head spin. And the lunch...the lunch was heavenly. Smoked salmon and caviare and chicken coated in something wonderful, along with other delicacies that were out of this world—there wasn't a jam sandwich in sight. And just when Candy thought she couldn't eat another thing Quinn produced a bowl of succulent strawberries out of the magic basket, which he *insisted* had to be eaten with the bottle of champagne that followed them.

'That was wonderful.' Candy blushed as Quinn sent her a mockingly quizzical glance from wicked black eyes as she finished off more than her fair share of the strawberries. 'Well, it was. I can't help it if you tempt me,' she said with sleepy defiance, draining her glass of the strawberry-tasting, effervescent champagne. 'I'm a glutton; I admit it.'

'Relaxed?' Quinn's voice was deep and throaty and made her want to purr, like a small well-fed cat.

'Totally.' She lay back on the sun-warmed grass, the scent of flowers heady in her nostrils and the sunshine stroking her face with its languid heat.

'Happy?'

'Ummm.' She was too comfortable and too content to even open her eyes. The past had gone; the future didn't matter. All that was real was the sunshine, the feel and smell of the soft perfumed carpet beneath her, and Quinn.

She felt him draw her head on to his chest, but she still didn't open her eyes, and when he said, his voice very soft, 'Go to sleep, little glutton,' she was already drifting into the mellow folds of slumber that were swamping her with soothing languor.

She wasn't sure how long she slept, but it was the feel of something slightly strange—alien—beneath the smooth skin of her face that awoke her. And then she realised what it was. She froze, still curled into the warmth and smell of Quinn, with her head on his naked chest—his shirt was open to the waist—and opened her eyes slowly.

'You purse your lips when you're asleep, like a small child.'

She gazed up past the tight black curls on his thickly muscled torso but she couldn't think of a thing to say.

'What were you dreaming about just now?'

'I don't know.' Her voice was a breathless whisper.

'Was it me?' he asked huskily. And then, without waiting for an answer, he began to kiss her, drawing her up to lie along the length of him as he took her lips. Her soft, full breasts were pressed against his chest, her belly resting against his as his hands moved down the length of her, and his breathing was as ragged and sharp as her own.

'You're so beautiful, Candy, exquisite...' He moved in one lithe manoeuvre that brought him leaning over her, and she gasped as she felt his touch on the swell of her breasts. His open palms moulded their voluptuousness and then the dress was about her waist and he had released them from their lace cups, his thumbs rolling over her erect nipples and causing such incredible pleasure she was shaking. But it was nothing to what she did when his mouth followed his hands.

She didn't know how to contain herself and she didn't try; she moaned, she gasped, she shuddered in an ecstasy of sexual tension and pleasure, her head turning from side to side in utter abandonment. She was swollen and tender and barely realising what she was doing as her fingers tangled in his hair, holding his head to her breasts as she arched against the passion that was consuming her.

'Candy...' Quinn whispered, lifting his head and kissing her again, his body tautening still more as she unmistakably kissed him back. 'Candy, I soon shan't be able to stop. You know what I'm saying?'

'I don't want you to stop.' She was past false pride.

'Are you sure?' He had raised himself slightly, shoulder muscles bunching under charcoal silk, and now she let her hands and mouth answer him as her fingers struggled to pull off his shirt with touching inexpertise, her mouth covering his chest in feverish little kisses.

His fingers moved to capture hers, but only to guide her as he helped her undress him, and then he undressed her, slowly, sensuously, careful to keep her desire high— he had seen the momentary apprehension in her face as she had seen the full power of his manhood and he didn't want her to be frightened of him. Not for a moment, a second, did he want that.

He continued to touch and taste her for a long time, carefully building sensation upon sensation until she was begging him, in small, helpless, guttural sounds, to possess her utterly. But even then his head dipped and nuzzled every part of her, her full, rounded breasts, her slender waist, flat belly and long, long legs. Her skin felt like pure silk and the perfume emanating from her skin was heady, and as his tongue and his hands pleasured her he had to remind himself, time after time, to control his own desire until she was open and ready for him. He mustn't rush her. It was her first time and she deserved all the experience he could bring, but his skin was burning and his body was hard and waiting was the hardest thing he had ever done.

When he did ease himself between her wet thighs she was ready for him, and not as tight as he had feared, and because of the hunger raging through him he was soon plummeting to his own summit even as he tried to do it gently, so as not to hurt her.

Candy had her legs locked round his body as she moved with him, aware even in her innocence of how unstintingly he had put her needs before his own, and now she went with him into a world of colour and light and brilliance as pain and ecstasy combined until she felt herself shatter into a million tiny pieces at the same time as he uttered one primitive, savage cry of exultation.

And then, as she continued to cling to him, he gathered her into him, his fingers stroking the small of her back soothingly as she drew in long, shuddering breaths against his body and felt the hard slam of his heart against his ribcage.

They lay locked together for a long time in the mellow sunshine and Candy was amazed—considering the intimacy they had shared and the things Quinn had done to her—

that she felt no shyness. Instead there was a repleteness, a consuming satisfaction that outweighed any diffidence.

'Well, now, little wife.' She felt Quinn's fingers at her tousled ponytail and then her hair was swinging free to fall in thick waves about her bare shoulders. 'Now you know how much I want you,' he murmured thickly, stroking back her hair and moving her so that his eyes could roam her uplifted face. 'Did I hurt you?'

'No.' And he hadn't, not really. And then, because she couldn't imagine ever being closer to him than she was at this moment, she whispered, 'I didn't think you wanted me, not in that way anyway. You…you left me last night.'

'You didn't think I wanted you?' he said incredulously, drawing away a little and reclining on one elbow so that the full length of his magnificent body was stretched out beside her for her eyes to feast on. 'I've done nothing but want you since the first time I saw you, curled up in the waiting room chair like a beautiful bronze kitten.'

'But you didn't…I mean, you never tried to…' She was suddenly bashful and acutely aware of her nakedness as Quinn's eyes narrowed and he shook his head slowly.

'Ridiculous child,' he said softly. 'Candy, you had told me how you felt about that side of things, the pain you carried from your childhood. What did you think I was going to do? Make you feel worse? Would that have helped? Besides, physical intimacy was not necessarily part of the proposal, not until you were ready at least.'

Proposal. This was still just an arrangement to him, not a thing of the heart. She shivered, suddenly quite cold, and immediately he reached out and drew her against the warmth of his body.

'I want you, Candy, don't ever doubt that,' he said huskily, his body hardening against hers in such a way she couldn't doubt what he was saying. 'I want you more than I have ever wanted any woman.'

She felt the surge of his desire against the soft roundness of her belly and suddenly she wasn't cold any more. He had never pretended to love her, not like Harper; Quinn had been totally honest from day one, and that was a vital ingredient for any marriage. But he had just revealed that she was important to him, and that was essential too. It would have to be enough for now. She had his name, she had his body, and if she could find the key to unlock the steel enclosure he had built round his heart then that would make all the heartache worthwhile.

She had to be patient. He was kissing her, his hands moving slowly over her satin-smooth skin as he stroked and petted her, teasing her sensitised skin with the alien feel of his own rough body.

He didn't know how she felt and she had to keep it from him, had to allow his feeling to develop naturally, without any pressure from herself.

His hands slid down her body and he lifted her buttocks up to meet the thrust of his manhood, moving softly inside her at first and then, as her face mirrored her enchantment at the pleasure he was inducing, faster and faster.

He could feel the small rhythmic undulations deep in the core of her, and he matched his movement to her gathering passion so that as their shared pleasure grew to an unbearable pitch they were together all the way. And then they were consumed by the fire and light again, floating away into another sweet world where sensation was the master and the past, the present and the future all combined in a shattering explosion that left no room for anything else.

They stayed far longer than planned at the farmhouse, and every moment was engraved in Candy's memory. Now Quinn shared the huge four-poster bed and she knew the bittersweet joy of sleeping beside him all night and waking to see his face on the pillow next to hers in the morning.

They made love often, and in the most unlikely places; Quinn was insatiable, and she matched him kiss for kiss and passion for passion.

They swam in Matt's beautiful swimming pool, which was housed in a big extension with its own changing rooms, showers, bar and bevy of loungers and easy chairs, besides an excellent gymnasium, sauna and steam room. Quinn opened the big glass doors at the end of the pool to the sunshine, and they enjoyed a barbecue each night on the patio beyond, when they feasted on steak and chicken dipped in herbs and spices and salad and baked potatoes.

They walked the grounds, hand in hand, finding new hidden idylls and little wooded dells in which to make love, and they laughed together and talked together, each of them confiding some of their own bitter truths and past pain. And yet through it all, even as Candy delayed their departure each time Quinn asked her if she wanted to leave and start the tour he had planned, she was aware he was still keeping part of himself from her. The important part. The part which Laura had damaged so badly when she had killed herself and their son.

He was gentle with her, incredibly tender and understanding in their lovemaking, wickedly amusing at times and gloriously sexy all the time, but he wasn't *hers*—not as she was his, if he did but know it.

And it made her desperate to stay on at the farmhouse, where it was just the two of them without anything or anyone from outside to interfere with their growing relationship.

She didn't want to be like Laura, she reassured herself time and time again when darts of panic assailed her. She didn't want to *own* or control every part of his life and say who he could see and what he could do. That wasn't it at all. She just wanted to love him and know that he loved her. It really was that simple.

On the morning of their sixth day at the farmhouse Candy awoke to see Quinn, clad in the short black silk robe that was his only concession to nightwear, and then only once he was out of bed, packing his clothes into the black leather suitcase he had brought with them. 'Time for us to go, sweetheart.'

Her heart leapt wildly at the 'sweetheart'—he had taken to using such endearments now and again, in a casual, easy fashion that told her she couldn't put any store by them but which, nevertheless, were painfully sweet to hear—and she sat up in bed, careless of her nakedness, and said plaintively, '*Why?* It's wonderful here, and I don't care about seeing the rest of the world!'

'Because, my beautiful little siren, Matt phoned first thing this morning to say that his wife's mother has been taken ill and they're arriving home tomorrow, and it might shock the kiddies to find a naked man and woman in their parents' bed.' He had strolled across to her as he'd spoken, moving with the fluid animal grace that made him twice as sensual as any man had a right to be, and now he sat on the edge of the bed at her side and ran one winsome finger round her right nipple. 'Such deliciously dark *rude* nipples,' he murmured appreciatively, before his mouth took hers, urgent and hungry.

It was another hour before the packing was resumed.

They left the farmhouse just after midday, and Candy felt quite bereft for a few moments as she glanced backwards until she couldn't see the beautiful thatched building any more, in spite of the fact that Quinn had promised he would set the ball rolling to purchase the estate.

They had had such a wonderful few days, locked away in their own private paradise where no one could contact them, and they had been completely alone. It would be different when they were living there permanently, of necessity the world would intrude and real life would rear its demanding head, but the last six days had been magical, enchanting.

She would never be so happy again. She pushed away the nasty little voice in her head that had caused a dark chill to run down her spine and turned round in her seat, her back straight and her eyes fixed ahead.

Whether she was happy or not was up to her, wasn't it? And, having come this far, she wasn't about to throw in the towel and give in to defeatist mode. All her life Xavier had instilled in her that she could do anything she wanted, be anything she desired, if she wanted it badly enough. It had been that mind-set which had got her through the first horrific weeks after the crash and enabled her to walk again, as well as empowering her to throw off the numbing effects of Harper's betrayal and the deep depression that had resulted from it.

Well, she wanted Quinn—body, soul and spirit—and she had already got the first part, which was something. More than something! She glanced at the dark, handsome figure at the side of her, his jet-black hair gleaming in the sunshine and his impressive body relaxed as he expertly manoeuvred the powerful car, and wanted him so much she ached with it.

He had married her on the understanding that the arrangement would benefit them both—socially and careerwise. They would stand together, united in mutual respect and friendship against any outside forces, and through the bond of good-fellowship and fondness carve a satisfactory future. He expected her to be a career woman, not the mother of his children; an excellent hostess and companion, not a home-maker who met him at the door with his pipe and slippers and shared all the highs and lows of his day.

And she would never trick him into fatherhood like Laura had done. Whatever, she wouldn't do that.

'Penny for them?'

She breathed in deeply and flashed a carefree smile at him. 'Just wondering how soon we can decently stop for lunch' she said lightly. 'That cooked breakfast seems like years ago.'

'You'll get fat,' he warned amusedly, with a swift glance at her slender shape, 'but I'll still—' He stopped abruptly, swerving slightly to avoid a large crow that was sitting in the middle of the road with the sort of expression that said, *My* territory, Buster! and then continued, 'I'll still do my duty as an obedient husband.'

'How very gracious of you!' For a moment—just a split second—she had thought he was going to say something else, but that was ridiculous. Love didn't feature in Quinn's vocabulary, not any more.

The last two weeks of their honeymoon passed in a haze of different hotels and sights and sounds as Quinn showed Candy most of Wales and part of Yorkshire in a whirlwind tour that left her breathless.

It was different from the time at the farmhouse, but then she had known it would be, and she enjoyed seeing more of the country that she would be living in from now on. Nevertheless, those first lazy, sensual days were engraved on her memory and became more precious as time flew by, although the nights were just as steamy, and they often didn't get to sleep until dawn was colouring the night sky in soft pastel shades.

It was strange returning to the practice as Mrs Ellington and learning to live in the apartment above the surgery. She knew it wouldn't be for ever—Quinn had put in an offer for the farmhouse, and his friend had accepted it, but Matt's mother-in-law's illness was more serious than they had thought and for the moment all efforts to find a house in America had been put on hold.

As the country plunged into a record-breaking July, with

the pavements hot enough to fry eggs on and streams and rivers drying up all over England, Candy had to acknowledge to herself that she was pinning all her hopes on moving to the farmhouse.

It wasn't that she was desperately unhappy with Quinn. Not all the time anyway. Sometimes she was deliriously happy, floating on cloud nine when there seemed to be some breakthrough in his iron resolve to keep the door in his emotions labelled 'love' tightly shut, but always it was followed by a definite retreat—one step forward and two back—and then she would have to act a part that was growing increasingly hard as her love for him grew.

The cats were completely settled into their new home, which was one weight off Candy's mind, and the pressures of living 'above the shop' didn't seem to worry them at all, although Candy knew the farmhouse and its surrounding grounds would be a feline—and canine—paradise.

Quinn had already offered Jamie the promotion to practice manager-cum-vet, with the apartment as part of the package, and as Jamie and his fiancée were getting married at the end of the year the younger man had nearly snapped Quinn's hand off, so fast had he grabbed at the proposition.

For the time being Candy was using the spare bedroom as her studio, and the fact that she had to concentrate hard on meeting her schedules helped enormously. She was too busy to brood, although always at the back of her mind there was a shadow clouding what should have been one of the happiest periods of her life.

And then a new and very real worry wiped out all introspection in one fell swoop.

Candy had been ringing Xavier and Essie every afternoon for a regular update—Essie had been due to have the baby at the end of June, but by the end of the first week of July baby Grey still hadn't made an appearance.

'It's too comfortable in there,' Xavier had informed her

cheerfully the last time they had spoken. 'Food on tap, no worries, every need catered for! A Grey knows a good thing when it sees one!'

But her uncle's voice hadn't been so light-hearted when the telephone had rung the next morning, at six a.m.

Quinn had taken the call, listening quietly for a few moments before saying, 'She's in the best place, Xavier; it'll be fine, I know it. Here, I'll pass you on to Candy.'

'What's the matter? Is it Essie?' Candy had shot up in bed as soon as Quinn had mentioned her uncle's name; she had been expecting the call to be for Quinn, who was on call that week.

Quinn had his hand over the receiver as he said quickly and softly, 'Essie's okay; she's had the baby, a little girl, but the baby needs an emergency operation. Here, Xavier will explain, but be upbeat, right?'

She nodded dazedly, taking the telephone and saying tentatively, 'Xavier?'

'Hi, Cottonsocks.' It was his pet name for her, and in spite of Quinn's previous admonition the endearment brought stinging tears to her eyes, but she endeavoured to keep all trace of them from her voice when she said, 'Essie's had the baby?'

'A little girl.' It didn't sound like her uncle's voice, and she knew he was trying to keep a whole host of emotions under control when he continued, 'She's beautiful, very much like you were when you were born. A mass of black hair and great big blue eyes; the nurses are raving over her. The thing is…' There was a pause, and Xavier's voice was husky when he said, 'She has something wrong with her heart. There's a long technical name for it but I can't pronounce it. She needs an operation right away, within the next twenty-four hours.'

'I'm coming out.' She didn't stop to think about it.

'There's no need. You're busy and—'

'I'm coming, Xavier.'

A longer pause this time, and then Xavier's voice was even thicker when he said, 'Essie would like that. She's...she's holding on in there, but she would definitely like that.'

'I'll phone the airport right away. Give Essie my love and tell her it will be all right. Oh, Xavier, I love you.'

'I love you, Cottonsocks.'

And then, as he went to put the phone down, she said urgently, 'Oh, I forgot to ask. What's the baby's name?'

'Rose Candice, like her big cousin. Goodbye, Cottonsocks.'

'Goodbye, Xavier.'

She was crying now, she couldn't help it, and as Quinn took the telephone from her shaking fingers and replaced it by his side of the bed she said bewilderedly, 'They've named her after me. I'm Candice Rose and they've called her Rose Candice,' through the flood of tears pouring down her face.

'Candy.' Quinn caught her to him and held her fast for some minutes as she wept against his bare chest, but he said little.

When she pulled herself away, saying, 'I must phone the airport and get a flight,' he merely nodded, his face almost expressionless.

'I'll arrange that,' he said. 'You go and have a shower and get ready and I'll run you to Heathrow.'

He wasn't coming with her. She knew she shouldn't ask. It wasn't part of the arrangement to sit and hold her hand— she was supposed to be the cool career woman and hostess with the mostest—but she found herself saying, 'You...you don't think you could arrange for Jamie and the others to cover for you for a few days?'

'I'd prefer not.' It was short and succinct.

'I'd like you to come, Quinn. I...I need you.'

'*Candy.*' It was too harsh, and immediately, as he glanced at her white tear-stained face, his voice gentled, but the darkness was in his eyes as he said, 'I thought you understood. I'm no good at these heart things, and I couldn't do anything anyway. Phone me to tell me how things are and I'll be waiting for you when you get back.'

He would be waiting for her when she got back. She stared at him as her lovely face paled still further. All they had shared over the last weeks and she hadn't touched him at all. Not really.

Well, she could beg. Or she could throw a tantrum, or use emotional blackmail, or any one of a number of ploys, but she wouldn't; she loved him too much for that. When he came to her, *if* he ever came to her, it would have to be because he wanted to commit himself utterly and for no other reason.

But she had been wrong in one respect. She stared at him, her beautiful blue eyes with their thick dark lashes glittering with tears. She couldn't live one more day, one more hour as they had been doing, without telling him how she felt about him. That burden, on top of everything else, was too great. And if he couldn't cope with how she felt then he would have to decide what he was going to do.

Her heart turned over and pounded madly. How did one handle someone like Quinn? She could only love him, that was all the skill she possessed, and for this situation it was useless. If she told him she loved him she might lose him altogether, but the only way she could continue in this impossible marriage was with a foundation of truth.

'I understand.' She swung her legs over the edge of the bed, reaching for her robe draped on the chair to one side and slipping into it before standing to face him as she pulled the belt tight. 'You've always been honest about how you feel.'

'But?' He had positioned several pillows behind his back

and was leaning against them, the dark curls on his chest emphasising his tanned maleness as he watched her with unreadable hooded eyes 'I feel there's a "but" coming on.'

She nodded tightly. 'There is. The "but" is that I haven't been honest with you. Not lately anyway.'

'Skeletons in the cupboard?' His voice was soft and even, but she had seen the ebony eyes flicker and she knew, however lazy and relaxed he was trying to appear, that the spectre from the past had reared its head again. Laura had tricked him into marriage and then used whatever it took to try and emotionally emasculate him until their lives had been a living hell.

'No, no skeletons in the cupboard,' she said quietly. 'Not in the sense you mean anyway. I am what I am, Quinn, and the person I am loves you. That's all I want you to know. I don't expect you to respond to that in any way, but I thought it was only fair to tell you. If you can't deal with it...' She paused, and then took a deep breath as she said what had to be said. 'Then we'll talk about it and sort something out. If you need to walk you are free to walk.'

'If I need...' He was stunned, he wasn't even pretending to be anything else, which was some sort of breakthrough anyway, Candy thought with dry self-mockery. 'How can you say you're happy for us to split when you've just told me in the other breath you love me?' he asked flatly as dark colour flared across the chiselled cheekbones. He was sitting bolt upright now.

'I didn't say I would be happy.' She forced herself to speak clearly and calmly, although her tummy was churning. 'Of course I wouldn't choose for us to split.'

'Well, thank you for that at least,' he said with cutting sarcasm.

'You know exactly what I am saying.' *Don't lose your temper. Don't say anything you don't mean.* 'You see this marriage as a convenient base for two friends living together, sleeping together and so on, whilst they each pursue their separate lives to a large extent. No heavy emotional demands, no needing each other, no expectations.' And no children, no roses round the door—none of what will make my life worth living when I want you so badly I could die with it.

'And you see it as—what, exactly?' he asked curtly.

She had told him she loved him and he hadn't even commented on it! She could feel the quick temper that went with her chestnut red hair rising, and silently warned herself to take care.

'I'm not going back on our arrangement, Quinn.' She could feel herself beginning to glare and tried to moderate her gaze.

'Forgive me if I don't see it quite that way.'

And then suddenly she understood, her love for him making her super-sensitive. 'You're acting like this deliberately, aren't you?' she said half to herself as she stared at him. 'If you don't acknowledge in your heart I love you it hasn't happened! That's it, isn't it? If we fight and argue it can all be passed off as a row, and you were used to rows with Laura. Well, I'm not playing that game! I love you, Quinn. I want to be a proper wife to you, to be everything you need, not afraid to ask you anything too personal in case I'm stepping out of line. I want to be there for you whatever happens—'

'Shouldn't you be getting ready?'

His cool voice was like a slap across the face, and in spite of all her resolve Candy reacted to it in much the same manner. It was either bursting into tears or yelling, and the former could happen in the shower. 'Yes, I'm going to get ready!' she barked angrily. 'And I'm going to see *real* people, thank goodness. Xavier and Essie have gone through the mill just as much as you have, but they weren't frightened to reach out and take a chance on love when the real thing happened.'

'And you're telling me you are sure what you feel is the real thing?' he asked with hateful cynicism. 'Isn't that a little presumptuous when just a short while ago you had set your heart on a glittering career without any emotional commitments to mess it up? Or was that some other woman I was talking to?'

'No, that was me,' she said more quietly. She would never penetrate that cast-iron barrier. This was pointless.

'So what happened?'

'You.' She looked straight into the familiar handsome face and said bravely, 'You happened,' and then turned and went into the bathroom.

She cried in the shower. Not least because she had reneged on every good intention she had had not to tell Quinn she loved him or put any pressure on him or ask him to change. But hell! Her chin lifted slightly as the tears still coursed down her face. She had never pretended to be a saint, had she? And he wasn't a little boy who needed protecting from real life. *She loved him.* It was a fact of life, and if she had to deal with it the least he could do, in the circumstances, was to bite the bullet and deal with it too.

She dug her fingers deep into her scalp as she massaged the shampoo into her hair and forced her mind away from her own problems to focus on Xavier and Essie. They were the important ones at the moment. Xavier and Essie and little Rose Candice. The baby *had* to be all right. Xavier and Essie had each suffered so much in their lives before they had found each other; she couldn't believe their child would be taken from them.

She was still thinking of her uncle and his wife when she walked back into the bedroom. Quinn had placed a small suitcase on the bed for her, and after quickly drying her hair and bundling it up in a loose knot on the top of her head she began to pack.

'There's a flight at eleven.'

She raised her head to see Quinn enter the room, making for the bathroom. She tried to think of something to say and failed utterly beyond a quiet 'Thank you' to which he responded with a curt nod.

And then, when she thought he had closed the bathroom door, it opened again and he said gruffly, 'There's fresh coffee and toast ready in the kitchen.'

The drive to Heathrow was strained, and Candy was sporting a thumping headache by the time they reached the airport. They had only spoken in monosyllables, and she didn't want to leave Quinn like this, but she didn't know what to say to break the electric atmosphere without causing another row. Had she lost him altogether? She tried not to think of it and concentrate on Xavier and Essie and the baby but it was hard.

'This reminds me of when I shot up to Essie with a bag so she could go to Xavier when you were injured.'

They had just entered the terminal and Candy wasn't sure if she had heard the muttered words correctly. She turned to Quinn, her voice a little vacant due to the pain across her eyes as she said, 'What?'

'Hell, Candy, I might never have met you.' He was wearing a deep violet-blue shirt and black jeans and there wasn't a pair of female eyes that hadn't taken a second glance.

'Quinn?' She stared at him. How did he expect her to respond when he said things like that?

'Come on, let's book in and then we can talk. I'm coming with you.'

'But...'

She allowed herself to be steered through the throng of humanity and in no time at all they were sitting in the relative tranquillity of the VIP lounge, a pot of coffee steaming gently on the table in front of them.

'Quinn, I don't understand?'

'You don't understand!' He tried to smile but it was beyond him. 'How do you think I feel? I'd got it all worked out before I met you. No more trusting anyone, no more loving, no more pain.' His voice was raw and as she looked into his face she was appalled. He was revealing the real Quinn behind the mask, and this man had suffered the torments of hell. It was there in the dark eyes, in the white lines around his mouth and the grating quality to his voice.

'Quinn, don't. If it's too painful, then don't,' she said with frantic urgency.

'I sat with him, Candy. For six long hours I sat with him and willed him to live.'

'Oh, Quinn.' She knew he was talking about his son, but she had thought the child had died in the car. That was what Quinn had led her to believe, more by what he hadn't said than what he had said, she told herself silently.

'Laura was dead when the rescue team reached the car, but through some quirk, an air pocket or something, they think Joe had a few extra minutes before the water reached him. But it wasn't enough.' He closed his eyes briefly and then, as she reached for his hands and moved close to him, he opened them and said, 'He looked so small and so beautiful in that hospital cot, in spite of all the tubes and wires. I couldn't believe he wasn't going to sit up and grin at me. He was warm and breathing, his eyelashes flickering now and again and his hair curled over his forehead...'

The tears were washing down his face now and she didn't try to stop them; she merely gathered him into her arms and held him so tightly they shared the same heartbeat. They were alone in the room but Candy wouldn't have cared if a hundred, a thousand people were watching. He had held in this pain too long—three years too long.

'Men aren't supposed to cry.' He raised his head, wiping his face with the back of his hand as he took control of himself.

'Hogwash!' Her voice was very firm. 'This western world has a lot to answer for, if you ask me. In almost every other culture it's perfectly acceptable—expected, even.'

'He was my son, flesh of my flesh; I would gladly have died for him, and yet I couldn't save him. I should never have left him alone with her.'

'Quinn, it wasn't your fault.' She gripped his fingers as hard as she could as she tilted his face to hers with her other hand. 'He wasn't alone, he had the nanny, and you had done everything you could. Sometimes, despite everything we do, the worst happens. You've just said what really counts; you would have died for him without a moment's thought.'

He couldn't accept it yet, she could read it in his eyes, but she would make him believe it, Candy told herself fiercely. She had seen him with the animals under his care and he was the most compassionate man she had ever known.

She pressed her lips to his, letting her mouth say what she needed him to hear, and then she was strained to him as he kissed her, long and hard. 'I love you, Mrs Ellington. I don't deserve you, but I love you.'

'Quinn—' she leaned back a little, looking deep into his hard, handsome face '—you don't have to say that.'

'I've loved you almost since the moment I met you, but I didn't realise it until Christmas Eve, when I saw you laughing with my mother in the kitchen,' he said softly. 'You were so open and warm with her, so generous. But it scared me to death, the thought of becoming vulnerable again, and so I lied to myself and you.'

'But all that about marrying as friends...'

'I lied.' He looked at her ruefully, one dark eyebrow quirking. 'It was sending me crazy, the thought that some other guy might muscle in, and so I lied to myself and I lied to you. Can you still say you love a man like me? A liar? A coward?'

'Quinn, don't look at me like that. I can't think straight when you look at me like that,' Candy murmured helplessly as her love for him rose up in such an overwhelming flood that she didn't know what to do with herself.

'I love you, Candy, you have to believe me.' The handsome face was deadly serious now. 'When you stood there and told me you loved me...I can't find the words to describe what it did to me. But the letting go, the trusting... I was still trying to fool myself I could have it all, but *my* way, the safe way. And then you said, when I asked you what had happened, that *I* had happened. And I knew it was the same for me. You had happened to me, and all the lying and fooling myself in the world wouldn't make any difference.'

'Oh, Quinn.' Her eyes were crystal-bright, her face radiant.

'You're the light of my life, sweetheart. My reason for living. I know now I have never been in love before, not until I met you. Everything before was just a cheap imitation of the real thing, but...'

'What?'

'It scares me to death, this loving thing. When I lost Joe it was like my guts had been ripped out, and now there's you...'

'Quinn, I can't guarantee what the future will hold,' Candy said softly, 'but I can guarantee I'll never stop loving you. Xavier and Essie have the real thing, and as bad as this with Rose Candice is I know they will be there for each other and come through it, whatever happens. We will be like that. I promise you.'

'You do?'

His voice was trying to be light but his eyes, those windows to the soul, were desperate and impassioned, and it was to the unspoken need Candy answered as she said, her voice a soft whisper that throbbed with love, 'With all my heart, my darling. With all my heart.'

EPILOGUE

THE operation was a complete success, and by the time Rose Candice's baby sister arrived, three years later, Candy and Quinn had their own child, a little boy.

He couldn't replace Joe, and he wasn't expected to; Carl William was an original, like all babies, and his proud parents loved him for himself.

As time passed another son and two daughters were added to the family living in the big old farmhouse, with cats and dogs and roses round the door, and life was full of love and laughter and joy, and deep, deep thankfulness.

Quinn told Candy every day that he loved her. He told her with his mouth and he told her with his body, and each of their children knew their parents had something very special together. They had love, the real thing, and because of that the blessing spilled over on to them, and to their children, and just went on and on...

Because love's like that.

Your Romantic Books—find them at

www.eHarlequin.com

Visit the *Author's Alcove*

➤ Find the most complete information anywhere on your favorite author.

➤ Try your hand in the Writing Round Robin— contribute a chapter to an online book in the making.

Enter the *Reading Room*

➤ Experience an interactive novel—help determine the fate of a story being created now by one of your favorite authors.

➤ Join one of our reading groups and discuss your favorite book.

Drop into *Shop eHarlequin*

➤ Find the latest releases—read an excerpt or write a review for this month's Harlequin top sellers.

➤ Try out our amazing search feature—tell us your favorite theme, setting or time period and we'll find a book that's perfect for you.

All this and more available at

www.eHarlequin.com
on Women.com Networks

HARLEQUIN® SUPERROMANCE®

You are now entering

WELCOME TO RIVERBEND
POPULATION 8793

Riverbend...the kind of place where everyone knows your name—and your business. Riverbend...home of the River Rats—a group of small-town sons and daughters who've been friends since high school.

The Rats are all grown up now. Living their lives and learning that some days are good and some days aren't—and that you can get through anything as long as you have your friends.

Starting in July 2000, Harlequin Superromance brings you Riverbend—six books about the River Rats and the Midwest town they live in.

Available wherever Harlequin books are sold.

HARLEQUIN®
Makes any time special ™

Visit us at www.eHarlequin.com   HSRIVER

Coming Next Month

HARLEQUIN Presents

THE BEST HAS JUST GOTTEN BETTER!

#2121 THE ITALIAN'S REVENGE Michelle Reid
Vito Giordani had never forgiven Catherine for leaving, and now, seizing the advantage, he demanded that she return to Naples with him—as his wife. Their son would have his parents back together—and Vito would finally have…revenge!

#2122 THE PLEASURE KING'S BRIDE Emma Darcy
Fleeing from a dangerous situation, Christabel Valdez can't afford to fall in love. But she can't resist one night of passion with Jared King. And will one night be enough…?

#2123 HIS SECRETARY BRIDE
Kim Lawrence and Cathy Williams
(2-in-1 anthology)
From boardroom…to bedroom. What should you do if your boss is a gorgeous, sexy man and you simply can't resist him? Find out in these two lively, emotional short stories by talented rising stars Kim Lawrence and Cathy Williams.

#2124 OUTBACK MISTRESS Lindsay Armstrong
Ben had an accident on Olivia's property and had briefly lost his memory. Olivia couldn't deny the chemistry between them— but two vital discoveries turned her against him....

#2125 THE UNMARRIED FATHER Kathryn Ross
Melissa had agreed to pose as Mac's partner to help him secure a business contract. But after spending time with him and his adorable baby daughter, Melissa wished their deception could turn into reality....

#2126 RHYS'S REDEMPTION Anne McAllister
Rhys Wolfe would never risk his heart again. He cared about Mariah, but they were simply good friends. Their one night of passion had been a mistake. Only, now Mariah was pregnant— and Rhys had just nine months to learn to trust in love again.

CNM0700